THE BENT PYRAMID

Printed in the United Kingdom.

ISBN	978-1-912079-85-8 (Paperback) 978-1-912079-05-6 (Ebook)
EDITING	Martin Foster Martin Locker
COVER	Andreas Nilsson
LAYOUT	Tor Westman

www.arktos.com

TITO PERDUE

THE BENT PYRAMID

ARKTOS
LONDON 2018

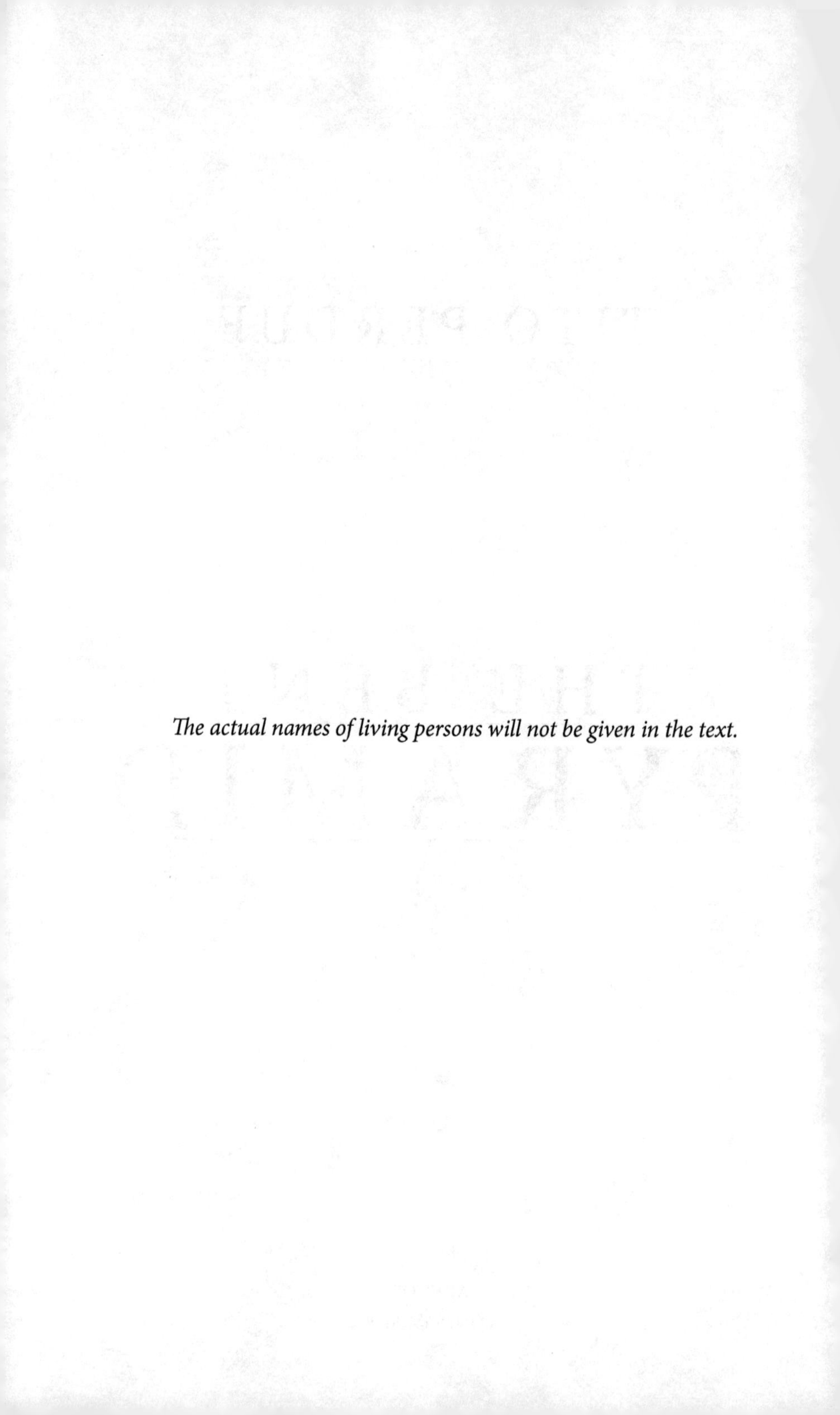

The actual names of living persons will not be given in the text.

ONE

In the mountains of North Carolina there survives a delinquent building of about 178 meters in length and 54 wide, an elongated configuration that once held that state's fifth-best joint collection of books and laboratory equipment. Venture far enough into the fog bound purlieu lying midway between Carthusia and Bryson City and you can be sure of a view of that rather incongruously situated structure in its present state of decay and extreme dilapidation.

Long and narrow.

Built into the eastern face of *Old Hag Mountain*, the building had been made to conform to the difficult contours available within a 40-acre rectangle lying just less than 6,000 feet above sea level. Approaching from the east along an overgrown pathway (too narrow for automobiles), it can be seen that the structure was provided with a series of narrow windows set at equal distances, as if the place had served as a prison or factory, admitting only enough light to notify the tenants when day had come or whether night was still continuing. The windows themselves were missing of, course, the little colored panes having all long ago been pried loose and taken down to Bryson City to supply the tourists and curiosity shops.

TWO

Among the last tenants of that building, (sometimes called "The Ark," and at other times "The Pile,") one was a recovered alcoholic from New Hampshire with a degree in ophthalmology. He had done all the things that could fairly have been asked of him, had married, had cured himself of his addiction, had done unpaid work in Pakistan, and by age of fifty-seven had become sporadically suicidal about conditions in America. All might still have been well with him, provided his wife hadn't left him, or if his son hadn't surrendered to the spirit of the age. In any case, he formed a bleak picture of a man on that day he presented himself at the western gate and in an expressionless voice applied for admission.

He was a well-dressed sort, prosperous, educated, and his discourse and personal address would almost certainly have qualified him for membership nearly anywhere else. Instead, he was ushered into the preceptor's office and questioned at length:

"Ophthalmology? That could be useful."

"Retired. And I haven't been keeping up with the literature."

Not strictly true. He had continued to subscribe to at least one important journal in his professional field.

"*Dommage*. And the money?"

"I can offer $700,000. Or a little more than that actually."

His total assets at the time were just above 1.4 million.

"Generous. But you won't get it back you realize. If you decide to leave us that is."

"Understood."

"All right then, good; now what is it precisely that you expect to find here?" (Called the "preceptor" by most of the fellows, or sometimes the "adjudicator," this was an emaciated person in a brown suit, brown shoes, and matching watchband who directed the affairs of the institution from a narrow office in the far southeastern corner of the building. Here, among books and framed photographs and two paired dogs snoozing on the floor, he spent his mornings at the computer and afternoons rendering snap decisions on the problems brought before him. A complicated person deserving a full chapter to himself, he could have told a great deal more about his life and experiences than he was likely ever to do.)

"What precisely is it you expect to find here?" the eye doctor had been asked.

"I want to *think*. I want to think, and then I want to die."

"Ah. You've been rehearsing that, no? Dying?"

"Been very depressed these last few years."

"Well of course. You must learn to enjoy it."

"I'd also like to have access to your library."

"That's not impossible. If you're admitted, I mean. But can you get along with people? *Odd people*, some of us. More importantly, can you get along with *me*? I can be very inflexible at times. Very."

"Yes, sir, I've heard about that. Sir, I can get along with anybody who's truly serious and knows how to think."

"And the others?"

"I avoid them."

"Good! Already I'm leaning in your direction. But I'll need to know a great deal more than that."

(The day was cloudy, rain threatening. One could hear the nearby sounds of the forest, and from much further away the almost imperceptible noise of traffic along The Blue Ridge Parkway. That was when the older dog [see above] raised his weathered head and glared briefly at the visitor who had left his chair and was striding back and forth in the tiny office.)

A moderately good-looking woman, she had fallen into slovenly habits before the marriage was five years old.

"I don't know what it is, sir. She was so beautiful when she was young, and could have continued forever side-by-side with me; instead her development came to a halt at about the same time as her body, and she turned out like everyone else."

"You're saying that *you* continued to develop, yes?"

"Why, yes."

"And turned your back on happiness. Can't blame her for leaving can you?"

"She claims it's my fault!"

"Of course she did! Everyone in this institution is at fault according to the usual standards. You might say we're the most faulty people in the nation."

"Yes, but..."

"To think is to be blamed; I would have thought you understood that already."

"Depressing."

"Oh? We tend to glory in it."

"Yeah, but..."

"Think of us as a hospice for conscious persons. Once we're gone, and others like us, a great calm will settle over the earth."

"Calm. I could use some of that."

Entered then a middle-aged Negro in a purple coat. Long time had gone by since last the ophthalmologist had seen this sort of servility, a graceful behavior that he would have liked to see more often. The coffee however proved just a bit too strong.

"Cream, please?"

The man ran to get it. It gave the ophthalmologist the opportunity to diagnose, as it were, the preceptor's left eye.

"Vitreous floaters," he submitted. "I believe that's the problem you're having with that eye."

"Good Lord. Can you fix it?"

"Well, there *is* a procedure. But I'd need my equipment."

(With cream, the coffee this time was much better than the original dose. Lifting the cup with care, the doctor drank perhaps twenty per-cent of the stuff before setting it back down again.)

"Could you fetch that equipment, do you think, and bring it here?"

"Much easier, sir, if you'd come downtown."

"Of course. But my contract doesn't allow it."

"Doesn't allow you to leave this place?"

"Doesn't allow me to leave my apartment. Except for the library, of course!"

"Right. Me, I'd be happy to stay in *my* apartment, too. If I had one, of course."

"What? And not have access to the library?"

It must have been the largest free-standing space in the world. Awed by it, the ophthalmologist set foot on the patterned carpet and for the first time witnessed the immensely long reading table that continued on for as much as sixty or seventy meters, before the applicant caught distant view of a bearded man turning slowly through an oversize book with the dimensions of a modern newspaper. Hospitable to silence and research, it was a holy place, so to speak, and had consumed, he was later told, more than eleven hundred million of the founder's original bequest. He knew, the candidate, that he was getting ready to go to the nearest shelving and, provided the adjudicator didn't forbid it, knew he was going to take down one of the gold-tooled volumes and look at it. As fortunate as he generally was in matters such as these, he had opened upon a good-quality woodcut engraving picturing a dragon, a maiden and a hoard of gold. Coming nearer, he thought that he could perceive yet another creature lurking in the depths of the cave in which all this was taking place. One could learn a great deal from such ancient materials, especially a person who had wasted so large a portion of his active years.

"Looks like a really interesting book!" he said, reporting back to the supervisor.

"Yes. Put it back, please."

"Whew! This collection must be worth a fortune!"

"Better than a billion we believe. The last inventory shows we have 62.2% of the titles in Burton's *Anatomy*, and 31% of Pollard and Redgrave. Like books, do you?"

"Yes, but I've never had enough time to..."

"Nor I. By the way you're beginning to impress me just a little bit. An average man, mostly still ignorant, who wants to read and die. Do you still visit your former wife from time to time?"

"Hardly!" He laughed. "She's in public relations."

"And son?"

"Real estate."

They looked at each other and then, as of one accord, broke out laughing from short distance into one another's face.

He was escorted (escorted by the Negro), down to the bursar's office where he completed two long forms and a much shorter one that gave the organization access to his money. A cherubic man with a symbolic key dangling from his belt, the bursar in a calm and reasonable voice then explained to him that his days of tax liability now were over. No one knew where he was and never would.

"After all," he said, "wouldn't you prefer your savings go toward books instead of foreign wars?"

"Of course. Instead of food stamps, too."

"Illegitimate babies? Salaries for elected officials?"

"Yes, and lots of other things, too."

"Publishers and television producers?"

"That. And public education."

The two men shook hands. The bursar's hand was large and pouch-shaped, a deformity resulting from having handled so many bills of currency over so long a time. The ophthalmologist couldn't refrain from asking:

"How about you? Are you allowed to leave the building from time to time?"

The bursar laughed. His mouth also was much like a pouch, a virtuoso organ for processing the high quality cuisine the place was reputed to provide. He was not just cherubic, he was fat.

"Why certainly I can leave! Someone has to go to the bank. Someone has to buy supplies. Someone has to pick up the pastries and dry cleaning, pay the electricity, etc., etc., and so forth, and so on, etc."

Waiting with decreasing patience, the porter then suddenly seized up the doctor's luggage and, never looking back, trundled off toward the apartments, a distance of maybe a hundred rods. A tricycle obstructed the way, also a few other children's toys scattered at hazard here and there. From one of the apartments the ophthalmologist could detect the undoubted sound of a violin playing in collaboration with a French horn three doors down. Here, midway between the musicians, the Negro stopped and began fuddling impatiently with the key and knob of what presumably was to be the doctor's new habitation. As of yet, he (the ophthalmologist), had seen none of the other "syndics," (as they were called), nor had he actually completed the sale of his home in Tennessee, a pricy residence described in a sheaf of unsigned papers lying atop his lawyer's desk. That money would be needed to fulfill his $700,000 pledge.

A four-bedroom dwelling with internet access in every room and crown moldings overhead.

His new apartment: long and narrow, like everything else in this unusual domain. Quickly he strode the length of the room and then turned back, touching each piece of furniture, dark, heavy, and masculine equipment that either were antique pieces or good imitations. Stained glass lampshades.

The adjoining room held two desks, one with space enough for a computer, a microscope, stationary, the complete *Oxford Dictionary* and a partial selection of Perduvian novels. By contrast, the other desk had nothing on it. Susceptible to high grade furniture — he admitted it — he tested the surface of this last-mentioned piece with his index finger. Until now he had not much noticed the half-dozen paintings, landscapes mostly, that gave the room a woodland aspect.

The following area was taken up by the kitchen, an ordinary facility with stove and refrigerator and a few framed colored prints of fruits and vegetables done in the medieval manner. He stumbled upon a fifth of brandy in the overhead cabinet along with a gallon of rosé wine. The refrigerator had nothing in it.

The bedroom was more luxurious than necessary and held a bed almost as wide as its length. He ran his hand over the incised headboard, a sort of pictorial "Braille" featuring a famous battle scene. The pillows were rich and deep, even perhaps a bit too much so for his already indulgent habits. He crossed the room to the wardrobe, a massy article in walnut or cherry, large enough for scores of suits and shirts and apparel of every kind. (In his whole life, he had never possessed more than a dozen suits all at the same time.) The room had a washstand, an obsolete affectation with a white porcelain pitcher on it. He sniffed the soap, an egg-shaped artifact with a far-away smell that really did put him in mind of a hundred years ago. That was when he threw back the drapes, giving himself a granulated view of the outside world, a crust of beauty framed against green mountains.

Battle of Kadesh (1274 BC). Unlike in Egyptian accounts, the actual Hittite victory was made obvious here.

He was tired. Tired from hiking such a distance to come to this destination, tired of interviews, tired of being surprised by such a number of things. He knew that he was going to slip off his shoes and probably his shirt as well and lie at length upon the inviting bed. The ceiling had a pastel freeze on it, a retelling of some old story of the Romans or Greeks. The last thing he wanted at this point was to set himself on fire with his cigarette, wherefore he snuffed it out in the painted ashtray modeled after the yawning mouth of a gnome of some kind.

He did sleep, albeit just very briefly, and then awoke to the French horn next door. He used the washstand (put there for decorative purposes only), and then rang for the servant. Day was fading and the bats were feeding. Time had come to try the "refectory," as that vital place was known.

THREE

He entered slowly, the ophthalmologist, a dignified expression on his face. Dignified, too, was the outfit he had chosen — double-breasted suit, vest, accompanying tie — for his first exposure to the group. He half-expected to be singled out for attention; instead the only person to pay notice to him was a bald-headed man at the nearest table. They nodded to each other. Came then a Chinese in an apron, a tall person for his ethnicity, who set before him a salad of artichoke and avocado pieces with green peas and cheese. Having chosen the proper fork, as he believed, he then began on the salad, using his best manners. Certainly he was not as educated as some of the members; he was however advanced enough to recognize Debussy's string quartet coming over the speakers. With music like that and food like this, already he felt himself to be remarkably "where he ought to be," and where "he should have been from the beginning."

"What! And never have a youth?"

A well-known and highly controversial historian and *litterateur* whose name cannot be exposed.

(This said by a wasted-looking sort of person sitting diagonally across from him, a man of at least seventy and probably a good deal more who had largely ignored his food to specialize on the wine.)

"Well, I…"

"Ignorance has its place after all."

"I suppose."

"You the new fellow?"

"Right. Yes, I am."

"Hmm. I don't remember being asked to vote. Don't care for the wine?"

The ophthalmologist lifted the beaker and drank. He had expected, correctly, that it would be a quality stuff. The man continued to stare at him.

"Woodwind?"

"Sir?"

"You look like a woodwind player to me. Am I wrong?"

"No, sir; I'm an ophthalmologist mostly. Or used to be."

[y]outh, the [ophtha]lmologist [h]ad briefly [st]udied the [t]rombone.

All four of his tablemates, their average age about 65, now looked up at him. A quick glimpse revealed that at least one of them stood in need of optometric help.

"But retired now," he said quickly. "Don't practice anymore."

"So."

Still intimidated by the assumed quality of these people, he only just now acknowledged what a fine cut of lamb he was enjoying. Potatoes prepared two different ways, cauliflower boiled in milk, hot biscuits with butter and plenty of fig marmalade, he must be careful lest he end up as plump as the bursar.

"Are the meals always so good?" he asked innocently, looking about at the faces. One man wore a bib, an essential garment for such an uncoordinated individual.

"Good as you want. We have a couple of fellows on bread and water."

Sequestered in a remote part of the building, these persons were rarely seen in public.

"Really! What did they do?"

"Austerity, you see. It's what they want."

Just then a woman came up, the first person of that gender that the ophthalmologist had seen. It is true that at first it disappointed him to discover a female in a place devoted supposedly to thought and the products of the mind; however, he soon changed his mind in response to her attractiveness and the way she bent down to let the wasted man whisper in her ear.

"He's asking if you'd care to come to our apartment," she said, addressing the doctor. "For coffee and ice cream."

In the beginning, the hue of the corridors was intended to bear some correspondence to the character of the intellectuals residing there, a policy that had to be abandoned when the population began to grow too rapidly.

Walking two abreast, the trio continued to the end of the "blue" (it was called) corridor and then turned into a squeezed passageway that required them to continue on in single file. Here the ophthalmologist encountered the second female of the day, a mere girl actually who smiled and made way for them. He hadn't yet seen, the doctor had not, any of that sex who even approximated to his own 56 years.

"Wives are accepted?" he asked.

"Yes. If they're willing to commit for the duration."

The man's dwelling proved to be rather more extensive and better appointed than the newcomer's, including as it did a massy hearth piled with logs. The three of them waited in the vestibule as the servant hurriedly finished with the vacuuming and then exited off into yet another corridor at stage right. The coffee was waiting, as also a bowl of various ice creams and a heavy iron serving spoon.

Confusion between Claypool and another member specializing in grackles and blackbirds.

"Claypool here is an ornithologist," the man explained to his wife. "Or used to be. And I may be the first one actually to have learned his name!"

"Ophthalmologist actually," the newcomer insisted. It surprised him to see his host reach into the woman's handbag and fetch out a long black cigar which apparently he intended to use with his ice cream and coffee. Pretending to be more at ease than he was, Claypool helped himself generously to two scoops of orange sherbet—it was sherbet not ice cream, the man had misspoken — two scoops of it and then lit up a cigarette of his own.

"And so you've been here quite a while already?" he asked, drawing nearer another of those little blue ashtrays that resembled a dwarf's yawning mouth. "I've seen the library."

"Yes. That will be our gift to the future, provided we're allowed to keep it."

"But..."

"Provided some 'Caesar' or other doesn't burn it down. Yes, and provided we can ameliorate the humidity in that place. And provided most of all that the money doesn't run out."

"The money?"

"Never mind, it won't run out. Truth is, he's got more than half of it in sovereign bonds, for goodness sakes!" He snorted, half in amusement and the other half as a punctuation element.

"The founder, we're talking about?"

"That's right, yes. 'Jones,' we call him. We'd prefer you didn't use his real name."

"I don't know his real name. And does he live here? In this building, I mean?"

"Lord, no. And that's the tragedy of it, don't you see. He has financed this gorgeous place, but will never be able to use it himself."

"Why is that? Not dead is he?"

"No, no, no. Ha! No, not dead. But he can't be here. Or anywhere else in this country."

The sherbet was good, rather more so than the coffee, which coincided poorly with Claypool's taste. Discouraged, he drank the stuff anyway, a token of routine courtesy. Five seconds went by while he considered asking:

"Why can't he visit here?"

"Doesn't care to spend his last few years in prison. You can understand that."

"Of course. Nor should he have to."

That was when the maid reentered by the hallway door, collected the vacuum cleaner, and then scurried off again in embarrassment.

"You were married one time, I believe, you said?" It was a woman's question, and it was the woman who asked it.

The ophthalmologist had said nothing about marriage, or anything else; nevertheless, he turned to the man's wife and answered politely. But mostly his eye was for an antique cabinet with glass doors containing an impressive hoard of modern books. Having finished the coffee, he had earned the right to rise and go to it, and get down on one knee to try to tease out the ex-professor's true nature from the sort of material he collected.

"Spengler?"

"Absolutely."

This was not a writer the ophthalmologist was terribly well acquainted with. "I've looked into Toynbee," he said. "Or the abridgement, rather."

"Oh?"

"Part of it anyway."

"You can't go wrong with Toynbee. He's another one who seemed to foresee just exactly what would be happening to us."

Suddenly, the ophthalmologist jumped back, astonished to realize he had positioned himself just eighteen inches from a saltwater aquarium featuring some of the oddest-looking creatures imaginable.

"God!"

"Hmm? He sees it as a kind of schizophrenia, Toynbee does. Me, I simply think it's the result of too much prosperity too far prolonged."

"Makes sense."

"What matters is not how you rank with human beings, but with the stars."

"That's hard."

"The whole list. Narcissism, the women's movement, forty-room houses. A supernal society would never have allowed the populace to become so prosperous."

He was listening keenly, the novice. It was precisely for insights of this kind that he had come to this place. The man had been described to him as the most intelligent member of the organization and therefore the most intelligent in the world.

Other candidates for that title were then residing in Poland and France.

"And just look at the professions! A country of consultants consulting with each other. My great-grandfather was a brick maker who built his own home. What about you, Clay, you rather make bricks or go about consulting all day long?"

"Bricks."

"Of course you would. And 'public relations'—what on earth is *that* all about? It almost seems as if these people, 99% of them, are content to throw away their lives on economic activity." He laughed. "We should be grateful, I suppose. The more they waste their lives, the more we can refuse to waste ours. That's why I consider it so generous of our founder to have given his whole life to trading in drugs and illegal arms."

By no means were all those arms illegal. As to drugs, some were illegal, and others much less so.

Claypool jumped back. "Arms!"

"What? No, no, you mustn't think it's an indiscriminate thing with him. He's choosey about these matters, and trades with right wing governments only." And then in lower voice: "He could have made a lot more money, lots, if only he'd been just a little less fastidious than he is. And we'd have a lot more volumes for our library, too."

"No doubt about it."

"Just think: without him, Latin America would be an even bigger mess than it is. Affirmative action, democracy, female movements, that's the sort of thing that might be taking place this moment, if it hadn't been for Jones."

"Certainly they don't need any women's movements down there!" He drank, Claypool, and sat forward fixing the former docent with his own almost equally reactionary eyes.

"Now when *I* was young, Clay—and I was—it was the boys who wooed the girls. That was a good arrangement for everybody. But today if they want attention—and they do—they have to provide on-the-spot blowjobs for any lout who asks."

"Oh, Herb." (The teacher's wife speaking.)

"My son, for example, he lives with this woman who makes a fine salary and seems to have completely lost her fear of males!"

"Yeah. I'm familiar with that problem."

"We'll have to do something about that, no? When the time comes."

The two men grinned at each other. Just next to him Claypool had perceived two large crustaceans of some kind dueling silently in the depths of their salt water aquarium. He tried to look away, succeeding finally.

"Just imagine Clay, what it must be like to live among average people and feel that you are just like them. To feel that you are "at home," so to speak, and needn't go on pretending to be stupid. A kind of ecstasy, I suppose."

A degraded (and degrading) aspiration endemic to lesser sorts of people.

"I know what you mean."

"Of course you do. That's why you're here. As for me, I knew by age fourteen that I wanted either not to live at all, or live among people devoted heart and soul to excelsior things."

FOUR

Left to themselves, the husband and wife began to do what in those days was most expected of married couples still in love with each other — change channels and/or adjust the volume just a bit. They were tired and near-sighted, and after six hours in the library would have appreciated a good old black and white film from the 1946-1954 period; instead, they were offered a comedy in which an unseen audience was laughing uproariously over a series of *double-entendres* pertaining to female body parts. Really, what sort of country was this? To answer that, they sat through a spate of advertisements presenting first, a tube of singing toothpaste jumping up and down. They sat quietly through an episode of talking peanuts and then a woman in a small bathing suit discussing automobile insurance. "And yet," the husband remarked, "we are allowed only a short time in which to live our lives."

Trekking back to the library, they took up their accustomed places adjacent to where government publications from all parts of the globe were housed tidily in manuscript boxes. Nothing could be more tedious than to transcribe and arrive at useful conclusions based upon the sort of colorless prose required of bureaucrats; nevertheless, they carried on with it, husband and wife, in their unobtrusive way. Nearest to them (fifty yards away) sat a raniform man with an old-style typewriter, a specialist in *Jagiellonian* literature whom no one in his right mind would wish ever to irritate in any way whatever. Apparently, the poor man had been in the same location for the last twenty hours.

Time was passing, a common experience that, however, had special meaning inside these precincts. Outside in the forest night birds were singing, deer were vigiling, opossums dangling from the trees. Further still, lightning would be striking out at sea with no one to see it. Murders were taking place, people shrieking in torture chambers, and while in Indiana, groups of youths were copulating gladly in pumpkin fields. Must indeed these episodes go unrecorded, no one to read about them later on? And anyway, what a small per-cent of things ever ended up in libraries in even the most propitious of circumstances!

They applied themselves to their research, the husband, wife, and some dozen other scholars unwilling even at this late hour to separate from such a trove of books. But is it really from such as these that revolutions are conceived and brought to pass? And are these in truth the world's most dangerous human beings?

Depend upon it.

FIVE

The woman had retired but the professor had not. Dispirited by the television news, he sat for a time in the dark, trying very hard to ward away the memories lined up two and three abreast to force a way into his head. He simply couldn't endure it any longer, the contrast between those days and these. And in short, he was one of a disappearing number still able to remember what life had been in a halfway decent country.

-1960,
king in
-1958.

He read, he slept, and then at just past 3:30, he left the apartment and wandered out into the forest. The climate was near perfect — it was October — and recent rains had cleared the atmosphere. He could see very well into Bryson City, where even now a few neon lights were sputtering weakly. Further, at an angle of about fifty degrees to south-southeast he perceived a feeble green lantern blinking between the pines. Truth was, the world was a strange place, and all about him strange people were fulfilling strange destinies in the night. Why for example — and this is just one example — why was the entire third floor of the *Burnt River Hotel* illuminated so brightly? Why so many owls tonight? And why had the clouds, my goodness, taken on such a dismal formation, which made it seem as if two great giants were hacking at each other with pointed knives?

Owing to a dinner/dance sponsored by the Lion's Club for oil war veterans.

He was pretty old to be giving such latitude to his imagination. Probably he ought to run back to quarters and lock the door; instead, he climbed a little bit higher whence the view of Bryson City was impeded by the topography he had reached.

That was when a breeze came up, pushing the mean temperature just beneath the range of what might be deemed close to perfection.

Landscape, landscape with mountains, landscape and mountains with green lanterns glowing in the night, this stood in place of religion for him. Save for the music of Wagner and Mahler (and a very few others), nothing else could better serve to bring him into touch with the infinite. Rather, it was the fatal *combination* of music and landscape that came so close on occasion, not merely to put him into contact with beauty, but actually to seize him up and rub his nose in it. It was, largely, what he lived for: driving by night along the Blue Ridge Parkway with Wagner on the machine and two or three serotonin reuptake inhibitors working through his system. He said:

Another instance of the eternal debate between materialism and wisdom.

"There really is another domain, dear heart, unavailable to ordinary people. Think of it like this, that some great artist or another has been privileged to peep inside a gorgeous mansion, and is reporting back on what he has seen."

"Or maybe he just dreamt it up," his divided mind suggested.

"Really? I tell you this my friend, either transcendent values really do exist, or life is but a hurricane of molecules that..."

"I think you've just put your finger on it."

"... that endures for just a little while."

"Correct."

"No, no, no; there just must exist another world, a wonderful place where all good things are absolute. But as for you dear friend, you can stay behind."

"That's good enough for me."

"Ha! Not even you could endure a world where mere human beings are believed to be the best of all things."

By 3:15 he had removed to still another position where a much larger town was remotely visible in the extreme distance, this one with a sinister halo that was continually expanding and contracting from one moment to the next, a "commercial" city he assumed, with harried people hurrying back and forth. "Prosperous and post-modern," he went on, "and rushing toward collapse!"

He was engrossed in these and similar thoughts, almost at times dropping off to sleep, when he discerned a tall figure trundling down the gravel road that led to Carthusia. In spite of the dark, the ex-professor recognized him right away as the man called Glen, a veteran of the second and third oil wars who had been left with just one eye and a left side forearm amputated above the elbow. Beyond that, only this much more was known about him, that upon his return from Turkey he had been set upon by a gang of Chicago youths and beaten nearly to death. Convicted of a hate crime, he had then served four years in the state penitentiary where he was ambushed in the laundry and raped over the course of two hours by negro gang members, a shattering experience that left him infected with the AIDS virus. Abandoned by his wife and daughter, he attempted to set up an auto repair shop in Raleigh, but soon was reported to the EEOC for having failed to employ the required number of female Caribbean mechanics. Fined $82,000 under the "tergiversation" law for moral incorrigibility, his photograph and biography were thereafter displayed in Post Offices and other federal locations in North Carolina and adjacent states. Released in June, he was placed under surveillance and made to attend a locally-sponsored sensitivity workshop taught by a severe-looking woman who detested the sight of him. He served (reluctantly) three weeks in community service and, then in August, learned that his remaining funds had been electronically expunged by a "progressive" bank manager responsible for ATM accounts. Having by then developed into an "ethnocentric" sort of person, as was said of him, he became the organization's sole member to have been personally recruited by the founder, and the only one to have been given his choice of apartments, a special diet, and twice-weekly visitations of a married, forty-year-old surrogate wife from Bryson City. No one doubted that he had deserved all of this and more.

A small sum, said to have been less than $2,000.

"Lovely weather," said the ex-professor, who had put himself in position specifically to speak with the fellow.

"Yes it is."

"A degree too cool perhaps. Not going to Carthusia are you? This time of night?"

"What time is that?"

The scholar consulted his watch, a largish piece of equipment fitted with an amplification lens for poor-sighted people. "Almost four," he said. "It would be light before you got there."

"I suppose."

"You should have taken one of the horses."

"Too much noise. All those hoofs clattering on the pavement. I tried that once, 'bout a year ago."

"Oh?"

"Yeah. Goddamned mother-fucking cop wanted to put me in jail!"

"Good Lord."

They had turned about and were ambling back slowly in the direction of the cloister. He had an odd gait, the soldier, owing to the loss of his arm. The professor's vision was weak, and the ex-convict was bereft of an eye; between the two of them, however, they were able to negotiate the uneven path. The breeze, meanwhile, was busily creating electricity in the windmill array that lay over against the western boundary. Together with the blades and the wind and the owls, discussion was almost impossible.

"... cocksuckers!" the convict could be heard to say. And: "... kill *ever last one of 'em* if I could. The children, too."

"And rightly so," said the scholar, paying the tribute owed by intelligence to courage. Besides, he liked the fellow.

SIX

Having passed through the vestibule, both men now submitted their prints and entered the main body of the building. It was late and the mercury was still dropping; soon winter would be upon them.

"Well," quoted the scholar, "I reckon I ought to get back to my place. My wife is probably worried."

"Mine, too." (He grinned)

"Ah, ha. How long is she here?"

"Leaving Monday."

They shook hands, each to go to his own place and wife. It would require the professor a considerable stroll to find the proper corridor, and meanwhile his arthritis was giving expression to itself in two quite different places. He moved slowly past the library but daren't visit it this hour lest he become ensnared by the place, causing his wife (and not for the first time), to send one of the servants to find him.

He had, the convict did, the best rooms in the whole organization, but had relied upon the whore to decorate them properly. The curtains were yellow and had the effect of emphasizing the color of the sunlight that for three of the four seasons tended to concentrate on that side of the mountain. He had a baseball with signatures on it, a signed photograph of a famous football coach, three books, a minimum wardrobe, and an enormous television set that had cost the best part of a month's allowance.

Truth was, he was the third-best paid member of the group. Nor did he have to use his own money for ammunition, gardening equipment, movie tickets, or any of the other debilitating fees routinely inflicted upon the group's educated members. On the other hand, he *was* expected to be available for emergencies.

And he was. No one was likely to forget the fate of a numerous crowd of Mexican migrants who had actually attempted to storm the place, nor what happened to the door-to-door salesmen who continued to show up at the rate of about one per month. Yet, he was remarkably generous to certain underground political movements that touched upon his grievances. Formerly an enforcer for a notorious association of oil war veterans, he had been given charge of an undisclosed arms cache — the reader is asked to make no mention of this — somewhere in Montana. He had been to Hungary on "business." Had assisted in the escape of a certain "assassin," as the man was called, condemned to sixty years without the possibility of parole. Had attempted an assassination himself. No one encountering this man in one of the corridors or at mess could fail to nod and, often as not, offer a salute.

It had been seen that he had just one eye only, and that the left arm of this left-handed man was largely absent. His hair was of a sandy coloration, shorn to unchanging length by help of his invigilating mistress. His other eye, the last one that he would ever have, was blue when seen from the front, and nearly every other direction as well. Called upon to do double duty, the thing had swollen to unnatural size. Finally, he was about five feet and ten inches tall and had a net weight, when his lost arm was imagined back in place, of something between 173 and 176 pounds avoirdupois.

It was this feature that especially engrossed the ophthalmologist's attention.

His clothes were purposefully the most ordinary part of him. (The last thing he wanted was for his image to be collated against the posters found in every Post Office in North Carolina.) Dressed in a hat ornamented with a half-dozen old Kellogg cereal pinbacks showing quondam cartoon characters, he tended to keep the bill down low enough to hide his glittering eye. His shoes, both, were kept in place with 32-inch laces that could be used for a multiplicity of things. As for the rest, although in general he preferred inconspicuous apparel, his ties sometimes bore risqué images. Except on Saturday nights, he carried no firearms on his person. He did have a Swiss Army knife with a blade, a corkscrew, a bronzed human digit, (seemingly a girl's), and a beer can opener. He carried a small Byzantine coin of no great rarity given him by an itinerant intellectual as a token of regard.

Issued in the reign of Justinian IV.

He owned a great many other things as well. He subscribed to a hunting and fishing magazine, and had a permanent prescription for his favorite pharmaceutical. He possessed a variety of masks and disguises, some of them for purposes of practical joking. He had an air pressure gauge (but no car), and a partial set of jewelers' tools. Had a tennis racquet and a yellow raincoat with a congruent hat. Had two paintings on the wall, one of a movie cowboy and the other a girl. And in short, he was precisely the sort of person who, but for his bravery and endurance, his enterprising nature, and the bad odor he was constantly offering to the nostrils of the politically correct, wouldn't have been allowed within arrow shot of the establishment. All over North Carolina, rewards were offered for information leading to his denunciation and arrest.

The man's roommate was a different quantity altogether. Possessed of some of the best-fitting sweaters on record, the exact location of her nipples, or "nozzles," as Wolfe had called them, were never in doubt. Her earrings were enormous, she wore ankle bracelets, and her ingenious brassieres had autono-

Now a ector's , only such ssieres known exist.

mous holsters for each separate gland. It was in this regalia that she tried, mostly in vain, to excite the intellectuals.

She also loved flowers and was ever giving little bouquets to members who had delivered an especially good lecture, or had helped in the garden, or been published by the institution's press. Except in bright sunlight, this thirty-nine-year-old helpmate didn't look a minute older than thirty-eight.

Inactive for the past four and a half years the organization's press had recently begun to issue small runs of some of the members' work.

Thursdays, these two often went fishing in the "river," or stream, properly speaking, that wended in and out of the property. The fish, such as they were, were seldom more than a half-pound in weight while their other dimensions were similarly abbreviated. The picnickers didn't care. The veteran had a guitar and the woman a basket with a Polish sausage and mason jar of lemonade in it.

ybrid creature, e "fish" appear have resulted n local sources ater pollution.

No one dared ask how to play a guitar with one arm only, and it was, perhaps, the very last thing his sleeping partner was inclined to bring up. Instead they spread their blanket in a shaded position where the woman was protected from the sun. Here, warming themselves in the season's deteriorating sun, the woman sang sweetly that old English ballad that the convict was most wont to play on his five-string guitar.

Birds flew over, most notably an indentured crow transporting a bored-looking toad on its back. After consultation, the two people had agreed not to copulate in view of the ark. And besides, she was due back home on Monday, where quite enough of that activity would be waiting. Shielding his eyes, the veteran caught sight just then of the organization's first chair stem cell researcher trundling homeward from a week's stay at Wake Forest University, where he enjoyed a certain acclaim. Further still, the convict detected two attractive wives or daughters playing badminton in the uncanny weather. It was late October and yet most of the colored leaves had stayed in place.

A person at that time of year could look forward to some genuinely serious snows moving this way from out of the accursed North. A person could now take out his blankets (a few days too early) and arrange them across the foot of his bed. A person could eat more rigorously, laying up fat against the climate to come. Or, as in this instance, a person could gather his lemonade and lie out in the weather.

"Does it still hurt?" the woman asked, tracing the veteran's prison scars with her finger.

"Naw. Little bit. Just when it rains. Sometimes when it's not raining, too."

"Does it hurt now?"

"Well, hell yes. Can't you feel it?"

He never really expected her to feel it.

She shut her eyes, trying to feel it. Suddenly, the criminal took her by the waist and pretended as if he were about to dunk her in the river. A man like that, it was impossible to say what he might do.

SEVEN

In Medieval times it often happened that an honored guest might come and stay a while. Not to say that *this* particular guest had ever been honored very much at all, apart from his reputation for projecting a certain personality onto the then non-publishable world.

He was a reasonably tall individual and his wife unduly short. Together they looked like two people of unlike heights. Nor did the organization roll out any sort of "red carpet" for the twain, preferring rather to offer the man a hastily drawn map to the nearest homeless shelter.

[side note:] ...t might indeed have been the ...earest, but still was six miles away across mountains and hills.

Dressed in shoes and clothes, the guest was given a quick tour of the 800-900 Dewey Decimal range of the 173-yard-long book collection. Having spoken complimentarily of certain of the titles and pejoratively of others, he was ushered to the refectory just before breakfast. He had expected to address the two or three dozen members who happened to be present, but was dissuaded by the preceptor, an adroit personality who coaxed the stranger to postpone that obligation. The stranger's wife, by contrast, was a much shorter and more contained sort of personality with a liking for crab cakes and egg rolls alike.

"Have you come far?" the adjudicator asked her.

She blushed.

"Come far?" he asked the man.

"'Have we come far?' Hear that dear? 'Have we come far,' he asks."

"Little bit."

"Little bit far?"

She nodded.

"It's these hills," Lee explained. "And you got more trees around here than…"

"We do have a great many trees."

"Well, that's all right I guess. Protect your privacy."

"We used to hope so. However, I expect you'll be wanting to move on tomorrow. See the world! I envy you, your spirit and so forth."

"Seen too much already. Say, who *is* that bozo over there actually?"

"The one staring back at us?"

"He's not staring back at us. He's staring back at me!"

"Yes. BTW, we're having a brief recital a little later on. String quartet."

"Really! Very decent of you. 'Preciate it. Just tell 'em I don't want any of that Haydn shit, O.K.?"

This "bozo," so-called, wa destined soor after his relea from prison, to win an international award for his achievements in Triassic paleontology.

They collected at the proper time in the music room, another of those long and narrow compartments that comported with the overall configuration of the ark. Winter was coming in, no doubt about it, and was producing a noise outside that vitiated the three several nineteenth-century quartets requested by the visitor. In truth, he was a nineteenth-century sort of man himself, and in temperament about as reactionary a visitor as the members could have hoped for. But he didn't much care for the looks of the cellist who shared no real comparison with his instrument and would have been better with a violin.

"We thought we had all the security we'd ever need," the adjudicator said. "How'd you manage to get inside?"

Discomfited to have this rather lofty individual sitting at his side, Lee didn't immediately reply. Worse was the one-armed man who leaned forward and in an evil voice whispered into the more convenient of Leland's two ears:

"That's right, and you can feel free to get your ass out of here any old time you want!"

Lee looked at him. He wouldn't want to tangle with this person and take responsibility for his vestigial arm and one remaining eye. Nor did he wish to undergo a beating.

"I'm thinking of leaving tomorrow."

"Well, all right! You're the man! Now you take care, hear?"

They shook, or tried to. The Shostakovich quartet (acceptable to Lee if not actually mandated by him) was in its best part, which is to say, morose beyond belief. Distracted by the miraculous sweater worn by one of the women, by the cupcakes and wine, the outside weather, and by the stridulations of autumn's last cricket, an evasive creature who seemed to have taken up nowhere in particular, Lee began to look about at the audience. "The last good people," as they were called, ensconced in the "world's last place," it was said. He had to decide whether to remain or not, and never mind any one-armed men standing in his way.

And yet, with his peculiar cast of mind, he was forever doomed to look upon human beings as if their skin was transparent, revealing to him an assemblage of gore and pus held together in cellophane wrapping. Really, was this the best the planet had on offer? A crowd of people with 428 collective exudates of liquid, gas, and solids? He wanted to vomit. With that in mind, he stood, brushed the crumbs out of his lap, ignited a cigarette, and left the place with an indignant expression. His wife, a much less persnickety person than himself, remained behind for the quartet.

He knew that he was going to the library, and knew that he would try to find a way inside. In confirmation of that, he sought out the violet corridor and, drawing up in front of one of the secondary entrances, managed to get inside.

It was grander than he knew, a gilded hall with ceramic tiles and spiral columns redolent of Sassanian days. He went immediately to the "sweet spot" in the Dewey Decimal system, and was about to pluck down a pudgy book with golden fore edges, when he took cognizance of the two, no, three readers observing him darkly from various positions along the eighth-mile table.

"Pardon me," one of them recited, a bearded man with a coruscated nose and scant hair. He had seen this before, Lee, how bald people imagined they could atone for that by means of a beard, or moustache, or by wearing a hat. "Are you a member of this organization?"

"Absolutely!" the guest replied with asperity. "Or soon will be. My wife wants me to apply."

"In that case," said someone from further down the table, "you will kindly leave our materials alone. They belong to us. They do *not* belong to you."

"Well I'll be goddamned. I come here, I'm an honored guest, and I know at least as much as you!"

"Quite sure about that are you?"

"Pretty sure. More than some of you anyway."

He could hear laughter in four different voices, a tenor, two baritones, and a child of perhaps eighteen years, said to be remarkable in mathematics. He could endure, this "Lee," the scorn of adults, not so of children.

"Listen, you little son-of-a-bitch, I'll take you outside and...!"

"Little? He's bigger than you."

That was true. Availing himself of the better part of courage, he turned away from this coalition and took down yet another book, this one a blue affair relating to the neglected history of the Balkan Wars. More sympathetic than most people to the plight of Turkey in those days, he read two full pages of the stuff before putting it back and then taking down in its stead a slender volume much more easily to be confiscated than the previous one.

He smoked, he browsed, he tilted his head to one side. Give him half an hour in this room with no one about and he could have taken over into his own keeping all sorts of rare and fugitive material, including some on vellum and at least one written in majuscule on yet another kind of substance. The collection held some of the strangest things.

er the dissolution and partial lestruction of this celebrated library, must be said that "fugitive" quality ecame even more pronounced.

In fact, he managed to smuggle just one volume to his room, namely that slender and aforementioned volume that when he opened it proved to have been unworthy of the collection in the first place. Even so, he had read the best part of an admittedly brief chapter when a tall and somber individual whom he had not seen before entered the room and took the book from his hands. Lee snarled at him, but decided against further action. That was when his wife came in.

Name withheld.

"Gracious!" she said. This room, it's…"

"Part of the stables. I don't think they want us to stay much longer."

"That's not fair! We're *guests* here. Aren't we?"

"I'm thinking maybe I won't even apply for membership."

"Yes! *Then* they'll be sorry they treated you this way."

"Right."

"But it'll be too late!"

"Much too late. Maybe we ought to leave right now."

"That's fine with me."

"But first I want to stop by the library."

And so thus Lee and his 5'2" wife. The weather had turned bad, and they had to struggle against headwinds emanating probably from Vermont and kindred locations. His coat, Leland's, had never been intended for winter wear, and never mind that he had amplified it with one of the institution's lovely pink blankets.

On permanent display at Columb University's main library.

EIGHT

The fifth person to be individually considered, the mathematical genius appeared to be more or less a typical American youth with an unhealthy complexion and the residue of a rather serious acne infection still lingering on either side of a nose that was too thin for normal functioning and that extended nearly to his chin. The ophthalmologist liked him, but the veteran did not. Lee, too, might have liked him, had not he already been excluded from this "last best place on earth." Nor could he understand, Lee, how a last place could ever fail to be the best.

Impossible to mention each and every member, even if they had all been as fascinating (and idiosyncratic!) as those selected for treatment.

worst, one ght just as nably say.

They had drawn off into the ex-professor's lobby, a much decorated chamber with portraits and vases, mounted arrowheads, two aquariums, framed displays of real butterflies, and Persian postage stamps. One could also have seen some of his personal credentials, his Ph.D. certificates (he had two), his license (now expired) to practice real estate, and a glassed-in "lawyer's" bookcase in which the boy right away discerned a boxed copy of the man's treatise on Bulgarian incunabula, his autobiography (covering just three years in the late 1970s), and his proudest of achievements, a massive meta-genealogy of seventeenth-century Calabrian seneschals. He actually drew this last-mentioned item from its place and was about to look into it before quickly putting it back owing to the docent's facial expression.

Additionally, the room held a collection of old silverware, spoons mostly, a diesel computer (now defunct), an example of

Mayan pottery which the man's wife had used for African violets, a laminated map wrought by Hondius the Elder, an athletic trophy for speed dancing, and then, finally, the wife herself.

"Would you like a cup of java?" she asked encouragingly. "Herb has told me how shy you are."

"Well if I'm shy, it's only because..."

The quality of her java was a frequent topic among the members.

"No, of course he doesn't want any of that sludge! The child is here to learn how to *think*, and that's the *only* reason he's here. Am I right?"

"Yes, sir."

"See? I told you."

"Oh, for God's sakes Herb. Of course he's going to say what he thinks you want him to say!"

"Is that what I wanted you to say? Hmm? Well is it?"

"Well, I..."

"See?"

"Anyway, he might like that sludge."

"Oh, good. The only person in this whole organization still capable of learning, and he turns out to be just another little..."

"He's leaving dear."

"I can see that he's leaving! I probably saw it before you did!"

This "barber" was later found to have carried on a subsidiary profession as an abortion provider.

The second occasion was on a Thursday just after the barber had left. Coaxing the child forward with flattery and chocolate chip cookies, the wife delivered him to her husband who had remained pretty much in the same position, albeit in a different room. Here the walls were comprised of stained glass windows leaving no room for the usual memorabilia and art. Settling the boy in the corner, the former professor bore in upon him, trying to uncover what other talents and flaws afflicted this most gifted of eighteen-year-olds.

"Been masturbating again, right?"

"Aw, Christ. O.K., that's it; I'm out of here."

The professor caught him. The child had brought two books with him neither of them worthy of the place to which he had come. (Not yet mentioned, this room also had a cabinet with a brief collection of primitive bamboo flutes in it and two somewhat more recent dulcimers.) That was when the former professor lunged for the cookies and in hurried succession choked down two of them. He said:

"You probably can't even imagine it — a tiny group of book readers, chess players and horticulturalists able to turn a country upside down. Say what? No chance of that? And yet they were just such persons as that who for good or bad took control of Germany, Russia, and France. And our American colonies, too, no? Remember, my innocent, that one good book can bring out a million troops."

"Wow. But I don't want to take over any countries, actually."

"You will. When you get old and see the rewards all going to golf players and debased people chasing the bottom line. *That's* when the desire for mass slaughter will fill your heart and turn your blood to lava."

"Not me."

"You must. Our democracy is in the most woeful condition and hasn't a chance, except for us. I am reminded of that famous *Bent Pyramid of Egypt*, that had started out so well. Look at it now."

"Yeah, but...!"

"Listen to me. In the beginning America was a more or less normal country with a proportional economy. Today it's an economy with the hull of a country chasing along behind. And to be forever getting richer, the leadership has opened the gates to every sort of stranger, whether they hate us only a little, or whether greatly. And therefore, speaking demographically, we have become everything in general and nothing in particular. How'd you like to be married to a person like that?"

The ex-professor was actually *understating* the plight of that one-time Caucasian society.

"I guess not."

"No. Think of it as the endpoint of democracy, where everything is equal and the value of humanity is divided by its numbers."

"Never thought of it like that. Well, I need to get on back and..."

They caught him. The boy was tall and rangy, big elbows, his shirttail hung out and his head was as large and as square as a concrete building block. The ex-professor resumed the lesson:

"Some people are just better than others. And what's the purpose of money and politics, of war and engineering, if not to build a scaffolding for art and genius? In the long run, nothing else matters very much. Why have we forgotten 98% of all human beings, but remember Greece?"

"Well, I reckon that's because of..."

"These modern follies! Most of them adumbrated by the horrors of integration, an egalitarian movement designed to hasten the dilution of race-specific qualities. What they really want, these genocidists, is a homogenized world requiring a destruction of the tribes." He halted then. Outside it had begun to snow, an event that "adumbrated," as he might have said, the much worse weather still to come. "How very fortunate for rulers that the people can't think," the professor added finally, repeating the words of a world-famous statesman.

NINE

The child had heard some amazing things during that first session and was moving back hastily to his own two-room apartment when he nearly collided into a well-dressed individual pulling a little red wagon behind him. Large enough to contain a piece of furniture as big almost as a piano, or a harpsichord, at any rate, a small one, the wagon was instead full of a wooden crate holding, of all things, books. They apologized to each other, the child and the older man who expressed himself this way:

"You couldn't help me with this thing could you?"

"Sure!" said the boy, falling in behind. He wanted to be as helpful as possible in the unlikely event he might choose actually to stay in this — he couldn't think of the correct adjective — this extraordinary place. Together they hauled the conveyance up the slight incline of the yellow corridor, continuing on to the library where the steward had put up a display of cuneiform tablets with attempted translations. The place was unusually crowded today, the result of a certain project under the guidance of the group's sole neo-Jungian, an irascible individual called Etienne. The boy and wagon master entered the place as silently as they could and had traveled a good hundred yards before the psychologist stopped what he was doing.

"Oh, I see. Pushing a little red wagon back and forth. Good, good."

The man with the wagon, a human oddity in obsolete clothing, showed in his face how annoyed he was. Suddenly, he threw back his lapel to reveal a

His clothing, to speak only of that, was reminiscent of the sort of apparel seen in the works of Rembrandt.

badge of some sort, a bright golden artifact that reduced both the Frenchman and the other researchers to absolute silence.

"Oh! Sorry," the psychologist emitted. "And I'm sure I speak for all of us."

"Me too; he speaks for me, too," said another man, a lean fellow who had done nothing wrong in the first place.

And so this "wagon master" was in fact the book agent himself, the fifth-ranking individual in the whole organization. The young mathematician hurried to take a look at him and to memorize his features.

"Jeez," he said, speaking just to himself. "Looks pretty much like anybody else."

"Anybody else my ass!" said the Jungian, also speaking to himself. "And just how many bibliomanes have you known who've been empowered to spend a billion and a half just on books alone? Hm?"

"Not many."

They hurried, the fifteen researchers and the mathematical genius, to give help to the agent. The back room was a dim area that held yet another fifteen or twenty thousand volumes too costly for public exposure. Here, too, was where the binder lodged, another little old tiny man, mostly bald, a "book wrangler" who husbanded the volumes and filled his time with restoring leather covers, oiling vellum, incarnadining capital letters, gilding fore edges, and subventing endpapers with his own personal art. Such items, altered beyond expert identification, had no possible equivalence in money. The seventh ranking member of the institution, the wrangler, had never been seen outside that room.

Not that the members, all save one, gave grounds for suspicion.

To open the crate, remove the padding, and then carefully to lift out the books one by one was a privilege shared by the buyer and sometimes the retired professor. The first title, it is true, did not at first appear to be of interest, not till the former professor opened the thing at page 119, his favorite number, and withdrew a 300-year-old piece of correspondence in a peculiar, very thin penmanship that ran off the page and, presumably, had continued over onto some adjacent surface. An odd business, it caused the binder to take the thing away and run off with it.

The next book was not a book while the third seemed to hold a French language poem of great length in which the writer had sought to extend the story of Daphnis and Chloe unto the next generation. The man called Toby asked to see it and having read a few lines, asserted that: "Among the clerisy, there are none so loathsome as those who imagine themselves poets."

..nown copy of ... rather ornate ...ume is believe ...o be in private possession.

The next book turned out to be a medieval hymnal of some sort. Intrigued by the hand-painted notes (musical notes), some as big as pears, the ophthalmologist tried to hum to it, a social error that kept him silent for the rest of this episode. All these books were to be added either to the founder's personal trove or, under the right circumstances, to the main collection, a priceless addition to what quickly was becoming the pre-eminent collection south of The Library of Congress and east of The University of Texas.

There was no question but that the book buyer had a predisposition for sixteenth and seventeenth-century material, and never mind that today many of these are available in electronic form. Electronic form? He would have preferred to bring together hoards of expert scribes supplied with quill and paper.

A tremendously ...sive undertaking, ...ming it had been attempted.

No one despised modernity more than he. His head was squash-shaped, his shoes were like an elf's, and his pantaloons were custom made. Strange stories went back and forth regarding his personal appearances at European book auctions. Jailed twice

Not strictly true. One could have named several others who hated it even more.

for illegal purchases, he had learned the underworld argot of Italy and France. His Latin, too, was good, very good, indeed, much more so than his familiarity with normal behavior and everyday affairs.

"Would you just kindly *get out of the light*?" he "asked" the botanist. And then: "Good God a'mighty! Who the devil is that one?"

"It's all right, Godfrey. He's new."

"That much I can see for myself. Standing over there. What does he want, for example?"

"He's genius, Godfrey. A real one."

"Doubt it."

"No, we've seen the scores."

"Maybe so, maybe so. But I don't remember being asked to vote."

"You were out of the country."

"Oh, I see; you waited till I was out of the country. Smart. So do I get to vote now?"

"Too late."

"Well of course it's too late! It always is!"

"Godfrey, Godfrey. You had your way, we wouldn't have any members at all."

"Now that is just plain... Watch it! Careful how you handle that thing for Christ's sakes! I had to trade my passport for it."

By 4:15 they had unloaded all the books and associated materials and had organized the stuff by order of color and age on the middle shelf that stood level with the eyes of a garden-variety human male wearing three-quarter-inch soles. Never daring actually to lay a finger on these treasures, the ophthalmologist, a man of somewhat less than average height, reviewed the titles on tiptoes. He knew this much, that

These "tiptoes" refer rather to the man's actions than to the posture of the books.

if ever he was to prove himself and show that he was qualified to be here, he must screw up his enthusiasm and, as it were, *gush* over what seemed to him nothing more than a shelf of old books in highly various condition.

"Oh!" he said. "And this one! Boy howdy, you sure knew what you were doing!"

The four men and mathematician turned to look at him.

"Don't recall voting on this one either."

"Eye doctor."

"I doubt it."

"No, he's a serious person Godfrey. Why so hard on him? And he brought $700,000 with him, too."

"Well, I reckon we can always use an eye doctor. My own eyes, for example, they... Goddamn it! Would you just *please* stop manhandling that poor book!"

It seemed the kid might cry. The book was his own possession, a blue octavo that he carried everywhere.

"It's *his* book Godfrey. He has every right in this world."

"In this building, *all* the books are mine. All. Provenance notwithstanding."

One book had been given false covers, a stratagem to get it past the cultural custodians in Lisbon. They marveled at it, each man (including now the preceptor, who had appeared from out of nowhere), each of them coming forward in turn. As if that were not enough, the "bad boy" held some dozen or more woodcut plates that showed in fine detail the actual appearance of the world in those days. One could see the acorns on the trees, the stars, the curvature of the Atlantic, the facial expressions of a milkmaid, and cow.

Not at all unusual in those days for exceptional objects, books included, to be called by this name.

"Those were the days!" the book steward said. "Just look at that woman. Dutiful and loyal, a life expectancy of about forty.

Tell me — come here you — you see any decadence in a face like that? What?"

"No, sir."

"Because there isn't any!"

"Not a whit."

"And the stars! They were so much closer back then."

"Which explains their great size."

"And observe the crudity of the workmanship, an index to the sincerity of the man who wrought it."

"It *is* crude."

"Perhaps his knife was dull," the eye doctor suggested.

The men and mathematician turned to look at him. It is true that another half-dozen intellectuals had crowded into the space jostling for a view of the new acquisition. Disguised under the covers of a late twentieth-century piece of New York rubbish, the import-export authorities in Portugal had not the slightest idea of what their country was allowing to slip between the long brown fingers so characteristic of that people.

"Because *our* country," the agent said, "is deteriorating at a somewhat slower pace than in Europe and..."

"Appreciably slower."

"... our library will survive longer than theirs."

"Quite right. Another fifty years and there'll be no readers anywhere. *Quality* readers I had meant to say."

"Maybe we ought to upload them to the machine. Just in case."

The group turned and looked at him. The agent had actually attempted this at one time before the courts had required computer networks to embody an equalities filter.

Adopted in secret session, this legislation remains largely unknown by the general population.

TEN

Refreshed by his inspection of this new addition to the institute's book collection, the preceptor moved briskly down the rose-colored corridor. He saluted and then moved past the two boxer dogs still patrolling that area after five hours on the job. He almost hated to go back to his office where some very weighty personnel matters needed to be resolved. And sometimes he wished he were just another member at liberty to read and drink and think about a whole raft of things.

No, he had to be lofty and strict. Had to wear his purple blouse at all times, and particularly had to keep abreast of the new theories forever drifting back and forth among the library, the corridors, the mess, and the apartments. Would they never agree? And would anyone ever actually *do* anything as opposed simply to mooting about it? And the founder, that sainted man, was he finally to receive any value in return for his donation — profits derived from the weapons he had sold, his hedge funds and real estate scams?

Almost as worrisome were the clashes among the membership, the hatred between this person and that, the never-ending argument between the Platonists who adhered to the idealist philosophy, and the materialists who gave no credence to anyone ignorant of basic chemistry.

Most worrisome of all (apart from an insane member who lived off by himself at the rear of the blue corridor) was the former professor, that atrabilious person who had taken the young mathematician under tutelage. Thinking of it, the rector took out the

Opinions vary greatly concerning the personality of this member. Adored by some, detested by others, no one denied that he had earned an elevated place in the organization. As to his wife, she was considered an unobjectionable person.

ex-professor's dossier, and although he deferred opening it, arranged it in the precise center of his organized, perhaps exaggeratedly organized desk.

The preceptor, or "rector," as he was also sometimes called, had a book collection of his own, which is not even to mention the half-hundred volumes on loan from his favorite slice of the library's special cache of rare materials, precious stuff that survived in minute numbers both here and everywhere. An accumulation of books surrounded by a mass of bright, brilliant, and belligerent old men — this is what it was, and this is what it was meant to be. Could anything be better? No, and when he took down one or another of those titles and, wetting his reading finger, made himself available to the wisdom of those times. *That* was when he might lift the phone or gear up his computer and communicate personally with other scholars dwelling in distant parts of the complicated building.

Like frogs at midnight grouped shoulder-to-shoulder around a lake.

He possessed a bejeweled eighteenth-century snuffbox used by him primarily for cocaine, had a twelve-inch letter opener with which to protect himself against the organization's one insane member, had a stand-up photo of a handsome middle-age woman who might equally have been his daughter or sister, a former sweetheart or his own never-mentioned wife.

A very partial list indeed of his real possessions.

He had other things, including most importantly a locked file cabinet overflowing with background information on the membership. He loved to pour through old grammar school records, childhood photographs, DNA evidence, citations and newspaper articles, Boy Scout badges, crushed roses that once had served for bookmarks, court appointments, books and articles published both by respectable and esoteric houses, personal neuroses listed in order of severity, stock and bond holdings, health, diet, languages, proof of Caucasian descent, affiliations, copies (whether purchased or purloined) of FBI reports, undocumented offspring, notarized avouchments of a dozen different kinds, achievements in philatelyin foreign languages, degrees, attendance at Bayreuth, favorite poems, Gail Russell memorabilia, grooming skills, (suits, ties, initialed handkerchiefs), and evidence of heterosexual orientation. All these documents had been laminated and their preservation guaranteed for five hundred years on the institution's escrubilator net.

Confirming that these materials were all in place, his pens and pencils lying in parallel, he summoned the Linguist and stared at him severely.

"And so what's the problem this time, Harry?"

"They turned me down! Won't print it! Me! I want you to punish them, Bill."

"Oh, my gosh. Won't print what exactly?"

"Won't print it!"

"What, is this another bibliography we're talking about?"

"Another? Is that the way to talk? This is far and away *the best bibliography ever done in this part of North Carolina*!"

"I don't doubt it."

"Seven hundred and nineteen pages!"

"Whew! Lot of work!"

"But that old son-of-a-bitch—what's his name—said he couldn't even *consider* it till next year!"

"The hound! Why next year?"

"Oh, they're still editing that business about artificial spontaneous human instantiation. Been working on it for three months."

"Ah! That *is* a weighty topic though, Harry."

"Possibly. But my chrestomathy of commentators on Heliodorus has more than *2000 citations.*"

"Two!"

"I'm just afraid one of those big New York houses might try to latch onto it."

To date, no large publisher has made the first effort to acquire the work.

"Mustn't let that happen. Hey! Maybe you should try *Arktos Media.* With them, quality is the only thing that matters." He reached for his pipe, but in his agitated state filled it with powder instead of leaf. He was tired, so very so, and meantime through the curtain he could descry three government inspectors approaching across the tennis courts. "Tell you what, Harry, let's put off your book until, let us say, February, and I'll promise you a printing of forty copies."

"Forty?"

"Enough for every member. And two for me."

It seemed to appease him. He tried without great success to stifle a smile that started out on the left side of his querulous lips but then disappeared altogether. "Well now, forty, I believe you said. Of course, I don't *ever* want to be a bother to you, Bill, as you know better than anyone. Like a thorn in someone's underpants. Or one of those pedantic types always looking down their noses. All I want, Bill, is to just *do my work.* Grinding away in my small apartment!"

"Thirty-eight hundred square feet. But yes, I understand you perfectly. Here, let me turn you loose now, Harry, so you can get back to it. *Scholarship*, right? Nothing like it in the world!"

Came then his next visitors, three government agents clothed in suits and shoes and light blue ties depicting, respectively, the federal, state, and local eagles grasping thunderbolts in their claws. The preceptor rose to greet them.

"Well!" he said, reaching out his hand before then shortly pulling it back again. "Huey, Dewey, and L… No, no, just jostling with you a little bit. Ha! Hear no evil, see no evil, etc. How can I be of help? Want a cigar?"

He had no cigars. He did have two chairs reserved for visitors and on the wall a good copy of the portrait of Giordano Bruno.

"No," the federal man said. He was a full half-foot taller than the state official who in turn loomed over the county's representative. If the little town of Bryson City was also represented here, that individual was too short to be seen. "I came here looking for *diversity*, Bill, but I still don't see any. Bring 'em on out here so's we can look at 'em!"

"I don't see any either," the state man added.

"Now just a damn minute! You can't expect us to have a bunch of diversity people here while we're still trying to recruit a critical mass of lesbians! One thing at a time for Pete's sakes."

"You have that critical mass?"

"Coffee? I'll ask our new boy to bring you some."

"I don't think you have any lesbians at all!"

"I don't think so either," the county man said in small voice.

"All this acreage and fancy-pants people. Tennis courts and so forth. I'd just love to put a new interstate highway *right through the middle* of this pile of shit!"

"I wish you wouldn't."

"What do y'all do up here all the time, anyway?"

Came then a really small voice from no detectable place:

"I tell you what they do. They sit around reading poems all the time!"

"Yeah, they like to read about *Shakespeare* and the rest of those ole boys."

"I tell you one thing, they aren't going to be doing much reading anymore, not after they get the new tax assessment. Right, Bill? No seriously Bill, what's it going to take to get a critical mass of queers and niggers up here?"

Although the pause that followed gave the syndic enough time to think of an answer, yet he failed to find one.

"You need more time?"

"I do."

"Two weeks then. And then we'll be back."

Administration was hard enough already, but it became even more so when the preceptor was visited by one *Abner Furd*, an insane individual harbored by the institution on behalf of the little etchings and ingenious cartoons that he typically generated at the rate of about one per day. It was also true that he had generated some considerable income owing to the patent he had gifted to the institution for a board game combining Russian Roulette with three-man chess. The supervisor stood still for it as the man opened his portfolio and showed three successive watercolors depicting the leader and his extinct wife in obscene roles.

"Very good, Abner! Anything else I can do for you? Apart from your handler and implants? Friar's Balsam twice a day?"

"Yeah, it's that girl. The one what lives with Glen."

"Oh, no, no, no. You'll have to ask her yourself. Sorry. Anything else?"

But it was too late for "anything else." The crackpot had left the room already and could be heard speaking to himself in the corridor.

Left alone, the adjudicator now also began conversing with himself in a voice that at first was soft and even sweet at moments but then quickly grew louder than he wanted. Beyond doubt, he would have left this job years ago but for the salary, the accommodations, the authority, the books, cuisine, egotism, and his view of the long sloping field that ran all the way down to Bryson City. Let him shift positions just slightly and the view was merely pretty, but let him come back to where he had been standing when all this began and the scene was ecstasizing. Why was that? Well! Because some perspectives approximate more closely to paradise.

His salary, voted by the membership, was just less than a million a year. It put him in a position where he could bid against book agents when they confronted one another at auctions. That money also allowed him to vacation from time to time at one of Norway's more ethereal fiords. It paid his son's tuition at *L'Ecole Nationale des Chartes* in Paris, France and allowed him to contribute in a large way to a certain very promising anti-egalitarian political movement gathering force in Klagenfurt.

ELEVEN

It was the case that the ophthalmologist had arrived in these mountains without full equipment. Lacking a razor, spare socks, and a good many other things, he had begun to think of visiting the nearest big city for purposes that should be obvious in light of what has just been said. With this in mind, he broke in upon the preceptor, who seemed to be talking to himself.

"I need to leave for a couple hours, sir. Get a toothbrush, a few other things."

"Ah. Who's going with you?"

"Thought I'd go alone."

"I wouldn't recommend it. These people have gotten good at recognizing us."

"Oh?"

"Oh, yes. That's how Charlie got hurt."

"Ouch! What happened to him?"

"Got beat up of course. Not that he wasn't already very strange."

"Gosh, they must really hate us down there!"

"You might say that." (He laughed.) "Actually, you have no idea. No, no, I can't recommend that you stray that far, not 'less you carry someone with you."

They set out two abreast, the convict and eye doctor. One of them had a frightened look while the other was full of zest. Over the past months a trading community had sprung up around the "Ark," (as local people had begun to call it), a substantial development consisting of a barber, a bakery, a saloon, a florist and novelty shop, and some dozen rented trailers for the burgeoning number of perpetual applicants. But they had not gone far, the ophthalmologist and his partner, before they began to be followed by a hungry-looking man in tattered clothing and distressed shoes of two different brands. The ex-convict allowed him another minute and then suddenly turned on the person, saying:

Few of these establishments still subsist, or in that location at any rate.

"I'm always ready to kill people." (He took out his gun and showed it.) "Anybody, anywhere, any time."

They cut through the tennis courts and then past the gazebo where a covey of blackbirds had taken shelter from the sky. One cloud particularly, a monstrous thing shaped like Croatia, seemed to be turning inside out every few minutes before then resuming its prior configuration. It had snowed again the night before leaving an inch of new powder in which a dozen or more of the organization's geese were distributing foot prints that looked like maple leaves. (Two others had preferred to go skating on the frozen lake.) It was cold in Appalachia, and could have been much more so but for the sheltering hills. A conscientious man, decently educated but always seeking better things, the ophthalmologist simply did not (yet) possess the sensibility that would have let him see these scenes *metaphysically*, a scarce talent belonging only to the former professor, the superintendent, and a very few others domiciled as far apart from each other as the building allowed. The eye doctor said:

Spotted recently in Arizona, the cloud had retained much of its original form.

"According to Plato, everything is just a poor sample of something much better."

"Oh yeah? Interesting. Watch out for them briars."

By 2:16 the wind had meliorated to the extent that they could travel more or less normally, one foot up and the other down. It was a downhill trek, the one to Carthusia, and both men had taken a full breakfast of waffles, grits, eggs, coffee, and toast with a choice of jellies. Further, both men had enjoyed a full eight or nine hours of superior grade sleep devoid of dreams. (It was the founder's policy that his men should eat and sleep well and feel free to waste time, too, if that's what they wanted.) Just then the hikers happened upon a deer pawing at the snow whereupon the one-arm man set off to chase it down, a characteristic behavior on the part of this somewhat juvenile human being. Already they could see the distant steeples and smoke stacks of Carthusia, a plangent sight with birds wheeling over town.

It formed a wistful scene redolent of the medieval period. One could see as far as Tennessee, not to mention row after row of poor peoples' houses with smoke lifting from the chimneys. This the ophthalmologist *could* appreciate, as indeed, who could not? It was natural, but dangerous to assume that every home and every car sitting on concrete blocks had been earned by manly labor. They strode past a ramshackle mill attached to a broken water wheel. The ophthalmologist was advanced enough by now to see how much more beautiful are old things as compared to new.

For a long time, Americans had believed that if a segment of the population had been doing poorly, then the individuals in that group must be very fine people. This mistaken but tender misconception has continued up to present times.

At that time, the town had more than two thousand residents, not to mention another five or six hundred who came at tourist season. They passed in front of shop windows decorated for Christmas with almonds and apples and candy canes. They stopped to critique a display of cheerful paintings wrought by the town's grammar school children. "My God, as utopian as they are, those drawings seem to reflect some sort of inborn genetic recollection of the 1950s!" the doctor said. "Better not to think about it."

He made haste to buy a half-dozen toothbrushes from an elderly druggist who immediately recognized that they had come from the institution.

"Yeah, might as well get a bunch of 'em, the man said. Toothbrushes. Going to be a real bad winter looks like, and..."

"Yes, it does."

"... you don't want to be leaving your cozy little rooms, right? And why should you?"

"We shouldn't."

"Big ole fireplace. And all that good eating."

"Have any chloral hydrate?"

"Chloral? What, you plan to *hibernate*? Is that what it is?"

The ophthalmologist paid, taking his change in candy canes. Never had he seen so dark a day, a pleasing phenomenon for persons of a certain sort. Had he his way, it would be dark for nine-tenths the time. They passed in front of a diner, but opted not to enter when they perceived the caliber of the people inside.

"Christ," the convict said. "Look at that one."

"Don't point! They're looking at us for goodness sakes."

Next was a tobacco shop where magazines and newspapers were on offer. All in all, the town was quaint, and the surrounding hills were worthy of a painter, or photographer, or one of those fortunate members with a metaphysical bent of mind. The shops, too, were wonderfully old-fashioned and the people, many of them, mid-twentieth-century types. (He tried not to think about that.) So why then was the reading material in this place so inferior to the assumed character of the people who lived here? He viewed six magazines with naked girls sitting athwart motorcycles. Coming nearer, he tried to analyze the motivations of one girl in particular, a reasonable-looking individual trying bravely to smile in spite of the humiliations inflicted upon her by some, no doubt, worthless man. The newspapers were worse. Events in Bolivia had deteriorated, requiring the president to resort to napalm. A mestizo in New Hampshire had been offended. Current accounts had improved between South Korea and America, and the "street" was pleased. Turning to the comic page, he learned that Dagwood had retired or, perhaps, was dead. And where, pray, was Mutt and where was Jeff?

He bought, the doctor, a pair of galoshes made in China. In this case the salesperson seemed to have some respect for the institution and those living there.

"Smart people!" he said. "Hard to get into a place like that, I expect."

"You have a stigmatism by the way. Your left eye."

"Damn! You folks are even smarter than I thought!"

"Not me," the convict said. "I just look after 'em."

"And four pairs of socks," the eye doctor requested.

It was a small town, and yet the choice of goods was as good as the world could need. The ophthalmologist traveled from counter to counter, amazed at the plentitude of things. He watched a crowd of yakking youths splashing through a pile of sweaters, and then next a middle-age woman experimenting with various kinds of rouge. Saw a discontented child, a blind man playing an accordion, a defeated-looking man carrying his wife's shopping bags. And yet, fifty yards further, the town had deteriorated down to modern standards: a suntan parlor, video rental, porno shop, and a computer arcade. The doctor had been a member of the institution for just four months this far, but already the quotidian world was becoming strange to him. Saw a boy with an earring and a ponytail, his face the very picture of stupidity congealed.

"If a man"—he was speaking to his chaperon—"if a man consorts all his life with monkeys, mustn't he become a monkey, too?"

"Talking about me?"

"Over there, for example. And that one! Can't be sure if that's a whore or a high school girl. I'm sure she'd give you a blow job, Glen, if you'd just ask."

"Will you wait?"

"Fifty years of feminism and now they'll do just about anything for a minute's worth of attention. Remember when they were 'hard to get?' What a triumph for womanhood!"

"Really coming down now, the snow."

They exited the place but then immediately came back to pay the tariff on four large tubes of local toothpaste. Outside they moved into a crowd of shoppers chatting gaily in the admittedly very pretty snow. Strange weather for the South; it conflicted with the doctor's memory of seasons past. They passed a wine store presided over by a fat man grinning back at them, his Christmas spirit no doubt fortified by some of his own merchandise. Then a restaurant came up, a propitious place with fogged windows and the smell of things to eat and drink.

Venison was served in this place. Also in the evening, partridges in aspic.

They seated themselves in a booth near the rear and used the time to judge the people, representative specimens, he would have said, of early twenty-first-century Americans. Some very bad music was coming from somewhere, but the volume wasn't so loud that they had to get up and leave. The ophthalmologist ignited a cigarette, forgetting at first to keep the thing out of sight. He had formed a sympathetic opinion of one of the waitresses, a worn-out sort who had lost the last of her youth and was responsible — it could be seen in her face — for the child, or children bequeathed her by her itinerant boyfriend or husband. Except for that, he disliked to watch people eating, an analog, as he saw it, to excreting. Was it just modernity he hated or life itself?

"Oh I see. Our people don't do any of that. Excreting."

"Have I been talking out loud? "

"All the time!"

They ordered, one of them, seafood, and the other lamb, neither of which the restaurant had. Trusting to the worn-out waitress, they asked for whatever the place had in good supply. The coffee, to be sure, was extremely good, and the two men behaved as if they intended to absorb enough of it to suffice them through the long winter months to come.

"I don't suppose we'll live long enough to see which of our fellows will formulate the thinking that could save the dying West," the doctor said. Actually, he said: "Wonder which one it will be. I just know it won't be me."

He lacked the spirituality for that hard assignment.

"I'd put my money on that feller with the beard."

"Doubt it. He's insane."

"That's what we need!"

"No, I think maybe the former professor."

"Too old."

"He *is* old. All right how about that stem cell person? He could take us all apart and put us back together again!"

"That don't sit too well with me. Whew!"

Their attention turned to the television and a news flash concerning the severe weather coming their way. One could search the world and still not turn up as many gorgeous girls as gave the news, sports, and weather. Just now it was a brown-headed beauty with an appreciable décolletage. Other good-looking women had been serving on the frontlines in Bolivia, their corpses, shown on television, composing a terrible scene.

"What we have here, Glen, is a nation of men who are content to be defended by women. Decadence can go no further."

"Oh, I reckon they'll come up with something."

They hated to leave the restaurant; the weather was so bad. Facing into the wind, they progressed for, perhaps, a hundred yards before turning and coming back to pay the cashier. Up ahead, two automobiles had tried but failed to come to a halt. Someone's hat was blowing across the road. It had begun to occur to the two men that they had an ordeal in front of them. Yet they managed to reach the city gates before the warden, an emaciated man in a hat and goggles, closed them for the night.

"Where do you fellows think you're going," he asked, "in all this snow?"

His voice had an authoritarian quality that tended to intimidate at least one of the two men. It was the one-eyed man who spoke up, saying:

"The Institution."

"The devil, you say! You won't make it."

"How come?"

"Oh, boy. O.K., never mind, don't listen to me. Just go right on ahead. That's right, good, good. It's got nothing to do with me."

"How come we won't make it?"

"Bye."

Slowly, the massive gates were closed and secured behind them. Once there had been footprints leading in and out of the city, but already these had filled with snow. Earth, blending with the storm, had become indistinguishable from everything else. The return trip promised to be especially difficult for the one-armed man, owing to the shopping bags he'd been delegated to carry. Even so, he had put himself a good twenty yards in advance of the doctor.

Third most severe storm since record keeping in that area.

"Why such a hurry?" the latter asked, cupping his hands to form a megaphone.

Dark! Be dark in a few minutes!'"

He was right. The snow was frail but lovely and had caused the world to resemble a whitewashed sea with waves in place of hills. There was nothing much to be seen in such surroundings, and yet the doctor still found himself moving his head this way and that as if to bring into better focus the assumed landmarks that had mostly disappeared. Anyway, the whole process of moving from one place to another had always been a problem for him. If he wanted to think about the past, he could easily do so, but if he wanted to be elsewhere than where he was, he had to rise and go there. Couldn't it just as easily have been the other way around?

They passed a crow who had expired from the conditions and then an abandoned shoe suggesting that someone had run into *real* problems. He hadn't expected that within a few minutes he would be seeing his own recent purchases also left behind in the snow.

"Seems to be getting worse," he called to the convict.

"'Seems?'"

"I'm wondering how long before we get there."

The one-armed man stopped and turned, and waited for the eye doctor to come up even with him.

"Remember when you used to write a letter to somebody and kept on waiting till they wrote back?"

"Why, yes. Yes, I do, actually."

"Well, that's what we got going on here, you see."

"Ah. The more you want something…"

"Right."

They moved on. There was a short interlude during which the snow was replaced by rain, a much more unpleasant reality that went down the doctor's collar and drenched the lenses of his self-prescribed glasses. But was it normal for so much loud thunder to accompany snow?

"Thunder!" he called to the convict.

Again the man halted. "Want to stay here and talk about it? Or maybe we should just keep going forward—what do you think?"

"Forward."

They arrived at the bridge, an antique structure that couldn't abide more than 300 pounds at a time. From his knowledge, the doctor knew that the institution wouldn't be far away.

TWELVE

They were welcomed with beakers of grog and then brought before the fireplace.

"Gad," said the old professor. "I thought we had lost you for good!"

"Good indeed," came a small voice from the edge of the crowd.

This from an irritable British historian who felt the institution had too many Americans in it.

The fire was green and yellow while from the mantelpiece there hung twenty-seven bright red Christmas stockings. Having emptied his cup and asked for more, the ophthalmologist turned to the professor and addressed him: "I was able to buy some of that tobacco you like so much."

"Oh, my goodness. Really?"

"Absolutely. But Glen felt like he had to leave it behind. This drink has nutmeg in it. Am I right?"

"It does. An underrated condiment. Don't you agree?"

Someone had fetched the ophthalmologist's robe and slippers, another evidence of the approval, or anyway the acceptance he had earned among these people. On the other hand, many of them seemed already to be losing interest in him. Craving further grog, he followed the ex-professor back to his well-furnished apartment and took up a place whence he could keep an eye on the many unusual organisms that populated his wife's salt water aquarium.

"They really do hate us," the ophthalmologist said. "Those people over in Carthusia."

"Well, of course."

"Does everybody hate us?"

"No. Most people don't know about us."

That was true. The eye doctor thought about those words, his mind ranging from person to person and country to country, all the people who didn't know about them.

"*Would* they hate us? If they knew about us, I mean?"

"Possibly. But what do you care? We have thick walls, and besides, you'll soon be dead."

The ophthalmologist jumped back, very nearly spilling his drink. "I almost thought you said 'dead'!" And then: "You did, didn't you?"

The teacher laughed cheerfully, a wheezing noise that was picked up by his wife. Between the two of them, the sound went on for a considerable time. Meantime, the weather had deteriorated still further requiring the institution's innumerable stoves and fireplaces to squander much too much fuel for this early in the year. For his personal usage, the professor had laid by a half-cord of seasoned hickory, chosen specifically for the bright golden sparks that material tended to produce. Affected by the liquor, the ophthalmologist then made a comment that wasn't really characteristic of him. Normally he was the most prudent of persons.

"You got fired, I believe you said. From your job at the university?"

"No, I don't remember saying that. But yes, I was discharged. And not once, but twice!" He laughed. "Aren't you going to ask why?"

"I might."

"Amherst fired me for owning a gas guzzling automobile. And then three years after that, I was relieved of my duties at Béla Kun Community College in Billings for a violation of the affirmative grading program."

There followed a long silence during which no further questions were asked. The ophthalmologist watched as the professor slowly and sadly filled his pipe with an inferior tobacco that gave off an unwelcome odor simultaneously with a series of weak explosions that, however, did no obvious harm to the instrument. The time of day was 9:15 at night giving the professor another forty-five minutes before he was wont to go to bed.

"You're... what? Fifty years old? Sixty? That's why I said you're going to die very soon. Another thirty years or so doesn't amount to a thimble full of piss compared to quantum time."

Forty-two actually.

"Well no, I suppose not. But I..."

"Hold it, just sit there, don't move, I want to show you something."

The eye doctor agreed to do so. The professor had taken a disc from the cabinet and after inserting the thing, manipulated it in such a way as to bring forth what seemed, and was, a piano concerto in the Rachmaninoff style. The music was good, no question about that, even if the doctor saw nothing exceptional about it. He listened attentively, however, as the professor, deeply moved, played it over again. He said:

"Nothing wrong with that, you agree?"

"I do; yes, sir."

"And yet you don't hear one-tenth of what's there."

"Well now, I..."

"You remind me of those progressives who turn their backs on today before they've uncovered one-tenth of what the current moment has to offer. Another couple of years among us here, and if you're any good, you'll hear all ten-tenths of it and become at last like me. This is what I'm trying to explain to that mathematics boy."

"I see."

"Where does beauty come from, after all? This is what began to interest me as I was becoming unemployable. This little piece has, what, ten thousand notes?"

"O.K."

"But just change them around a little bit and there's no beauty at all. Isn't that odd? What's the difference between one arrangement and another, except insofar as one of them approximates to something even better? No, no, I'm not suggesting you should care about music. I'm suggesting you should care about that 'something better.' Give Plato credit for this."

"I sure will. Well! I'd best leave you alone just now to get your sleep. That was a good drink, boy howdy, and I just might be coming back for more!" He snickered, doing it without accompaniment. One of the sea creatures had slowly been devouring one of its peers over the past minute, and together with the grog, young Claypool found himself in a situation in which he was close to fainting.

An unsuccessful effort as it turned out. Within a short time the creature had actually vomited his victim, (who had remained preternaturally calm during the experience), back out into the surrounding element.

THIRTEEN

He hastened back to his own quarters, the novice did. It is true that he lacked the specific concerto referenced above, but he did have other music that was just as good. Quickly, he rummaged among his discs (organized alphabetically by date), and pulled out a handsome album cover with a reproduction on the cover of a Mughal miniature from Aurangzeb's reign. This was a pretty good moment for him; he was learning a great deal and the darkness on this night was more than just the absence of light. It was something in its own right.

The original housed in the Victoria and Albert Museum in London.

He listened for a total of, perhaps, twenty-five minutes till his extreme exhaustion mandated that he go over into his sleeping clothes, puff up the pillow, and stretch out to his full length of 5'9". The other members, most of them, were taller than that, and yet he expected to increase by other "inches," so to speak, as his soul and imagination, not to put too fine a point on it, put on further growth, as it were. (Not that he imagined there could be any change in his physical person which had pretty well "congealed" as far back as when he was nineteen.)

He dreamt that he had read every single volume in the organization's enormous library and was just finishing up with the project, when suddenly he came awake more exhausted than ever. Going to the door, he spied down the hall, finding one of the dogs asleep on the job. Nor were there any exterior shadows on his paisley curtains. His intention was to dream again, this time assigning himself a much briefer list of books to read. Instead, he discovered himself caught in battle on the American frontier of about 1780, or '82, with red Indians all about. Luckily, he had found some protection behind a downed oak whence he could fire at the enemy with very little chance that he himself might be hit.

Could anything be more delicious than to look out in perfect safety upon wild chaos in every direction? No, but when he tried to go on with this, he found instead he was staring from about three inches away into the face of his estranged wife.

She hadn't aged as much as might have been expected. Always good with make-up and its magical powers, she had made herself as pretty, almost, as when she was young. He could feel a resurgence of his ancient hatred coming back again. Even so, he had no wish to dredge up those old-time complaints now that he had finally begun to make real progress toward forgetting about the bitch.

It was now almost two o'clock in the morning, January 14th. One single remedy remained to him if he wished to sleep before morning came. Sitting on the edge of the bed, he smoked one and a half cigarettes and then drew to himself an introductory text to particle physics, a fascinating science that could be counted upon to render him unconscious at last.

He dreamt that he was climbing through the coils and pitfalls of a monstrous molecule larger than the world. This was followed by a very decent sleep of possibly two hours, a prenatal experience so sweet and lush that he would have preferred to persevere with it. Meantime, he was debating whether it were absolutely necessary that he rise and visit the bathroom, or whether to sleep again. That was when something happened.

He assumed at first that some of the local authorities had broken into the place and were in stage of placing people under arrest. The members, some in pajamas and some in clothes, had left their rooms and were standing about with appalled expressions. Himself, the ophthalmologist, had thrown himself into his trousers and was thinking of escaping out the window when he heard what sounded like bare feet racing down the hall. But how likely was it that any official within *his* experience of these sorts of people, how likely that they would go on raids with naked feet?

He fell in behind but could not stay even with his nearest neighbor, an internationally known film historian known to the group as Andrew Martin. To reiterate, something *was* happening, happening at the intersection of the green and yellow corridors where the dogs had their billet. Going back for his cigarettes and slippers, the eye doctor made a shortcut via a maroon but mostly untenanted hallway reserved for the ——— who so far had declined to join the organization.

That was when he saw the person. Older than he had expected, and smaller, and poorly dressed, the ophthalmologist was hard pressed to admit that this could actually be one of the country's premier stock manipulators. He went forward to shake hands with the person, but then drew back so that both of them could examine each other up and down. Possessing larger funds than the whole of Kirgizstan, the founder had mud on his shoes, snow on his hat, and a sprig of rosemary in his boutonniere. Hoping to evade the tax authorities, he had come (as Claypool later learned), by way of Portland, Sacramento, El Paso, and numerous other stations famous for allowing illegal interlopers in return for small gratuities to move back and forth across the country.

"Ha. So you're the ear, eyes, nose, and throat person! Good to see you again."

They shook hands. The agent had a somewhat greenish complexion, the inevitable result, one had to suppose, of so many years of handling bills of money. No one knew the true name of this person, or if one or another of his pseudonyms might have any basis in fact.

Fifteen years after this man's death, further pseudonyms were still coming to the attention of the I.R.S.

"Call me Jones," the billionaire said. "What the hell."

"Yes, sir. We always do."

"No wait, I've changed my mind. Call me 'sir,' if you would. That would be better, I think."

That was when a motorized serving cart was brought into their midst, providing the intellectuals with a choice of alcoholic beverages of various strength. The ex-professor chose undiluted bourbon and set to work on it right away. One could read a lot into the character of these people according to their choice of drink.

"What would you have, sir?" someone asked the founder.

"O, I don't know. Absinth, I suppose."

They had to run to the storeroom for it, a prohibited stuff punishable at rates parallel with those for the possession of tobacco products.

"Did you come to view the library, sir?" the philologist asked. "See what we've done to it? New shelving? And all the wonderful things that Sam" (the book agent's name, also an incognito) "has found?"

"In due time. In due time. Just now I'm wondering if I'm going to be given any absinth or not."

That was when the electricity went out. The storm had greatly intensified, producing hills of granulated snow that looked like sand, or like grits rather, or like a new species of snow overly-influenced by industrial

They naturally believed the loss of electricity was owing to the storm. Not for 48 hours did they realize it was a governmental decision.

wastes emanating from Ashville. The members were entranced by how quickly the stuff had climbed to the windows and actually threatened to seal off any usable view of the outside world. This was how Claypool liked it, this look of things at the world's last days. Already the moon had mostly been eaten away leaving just one bright spot not much larger than a distant star.

Far from "eaten away," the moon reappeared in full two days later.

"End of the world!" he said, jubilantly.

"Patience, Clay. Patience."

"I'm wondering if I'm going to be invited to sit down somewhere," the founder said. "Hey, what happened to the lights?"

It was likely the man's satchel was full of good things. Moving as expeditiously as possible in the dim, the group escorted their benefactor to the great room and sat him down in an upholstered chair that was conspicuously too big for the person. The members came forward, congregating about the man.

"Absinth," he said.

A fire was burning brightly in the hearth, providing only enough light that the members could at least see each other. The former professor, whose name was known as "Herb," appeared to be in an elevated state of mind. Compassed by some two score of the world's finest people, he fixed upon their silhouettes, listened to low voices, enjoyed the glow of their cigarettes. Yes, and someday they shall have all turned into pure thought leaving behind all sorts of theories for the betterment of literature and philosophy. The preceptor addressed their benefactor:

"How on earth did you do it, sir? Get past the border guards?"

The old man could not but laugh. "I cheated."

"Sir?"

"Presented myself as Hispanic."

They laughed, the crowd, and made admiring comments. Two of the members had brought carbide lamps that made their silhouettes look even odder than the original people. Seen from above, one would have thought the members consisted of creatures from outer space. One man had the strangest head.

"You'll be happy to know, sir, that we now have the second best Slavic literature collection in the whole state."

With particular strength in Serbo-Croatian.

"Oh, yes? I'm glad."

"Enough intellectual equipment to turn the world upside down,"

"Too bad we'll not live to see it."

"Karl here," (the young mathematics genius) "*he* might live to see it."

"Doubt it. No, it needs a long, long time to overthrow a society as deluded as this one, never mind how decadent."

"And yet, things can happen very quickly once they start. The Soviet Union for one example."

"True. But they weren't as debased as us."

"Say what? They were in absolute despair over there for goodness sakes!"

"That's why they weren't as debased as us."

Laughter.

"Absinth? Please?"

"Decadence is worse than despair?"

"A thousand-fold so."

"Maybe so, maybe so. After all, I haven't left the building in seven years. So how could I know?"

The founder asked for silence. "Gentlemen!" he said. "I have a reason for my visit."

They watched with extreme interest as the octogenarian opened his satchel, drew back a sheet of brown paper, and exposed a crowded hoard of what looked like high-denomination bills. The crowd moaned, though not with disapproval.

"Other people," the old man said, "would buy Senators or rappers if they aspired to turn the world inside out. Us, we buy wisdom."

"Exactly right!"

"Someone has to do it." (Turn the world inside out.) "So let it be..." (He rose and went forward and touched one of the members at random, the insane man unfortunately.) "... *this* one!"

All evidence notwithstanding, the members continued to hope for this man's recovery.

"Bad choice, Jones. 'Sir,' I mean."

"After all, revolutions needn't be bloody. In the long run, they always take place inside the skulls of persuadable men. And that's all I ever wanted really—to catalyze the intellectual basis for the next cycle of western history. No more a society that throws old shoes away instead of having them repaired."

"Right! That's our credo, sir," submitted Toby, an obsequious sort of person who enjoyed scant popularity among the group. "Any country that throws those shoes away is already on death's agenda."

"'Death's agenda!' I was *sure* I was the inventor of that phrase."

"Remember," the old man explained, "I didn't bring you here so you could toast marshmallows and love each other quite a lot. Or join hands and sing folk songs on the mountain tops. Better if you didn't have much to do with each other. After all, everybody is more or less disgusting in the final analysis. And then, too, we shall all of us soon have reverted back to the seawater we originally were."

"Grim. But something to think about certainly." (Toby)

"On the other hand..."

They waited for the founder's next words.

"... some systems really are better than others, even if the masses never change. Can you see Aristides hanging around a topless bar? Or Héloise reading a movie magazine? Not in a pig's ass will ever you see that!"

"Correct. Some systems are just better than others."

"Do you think I could have earned, or acquired rather, as much money as I have without the aid of a system as rotten as ours? In my whole life I never won a *single battle on civilization's behalf.* Which is why I'm relying on you."

"He tells it like it is."

"Of course I'm not ready to say that rewards are *always* meted out counter proportionately to human quality. Oh, oh, wait a minute." (He paused a few seconds.) "Hmmm. Yes, by God, I *am* ready to say that!"

"Me, too; I always say it. For example, I know of a pornographic actress who makes more money in twenty minutes than my daddy in his whole life."

Especially notorious was her performance with a certain hockey star in which she had introduced a new and highly innovative buccal procedure.

"Her name?" the one-armed man asked.

It was a pretty good discussion that could have been better, had they not already come to the end of the wine. Someone broke the silence. "I'm wondering how many tons of snow have piled up on the roof by now."

"Can only get worse. This is what happens when those volcanoes down in Alabama all go off at the same time. All that ejecta and so forth."

"Can't even see out the windows anymore!"

"Good. No one can see in."

"He's right. The Chinese, to give just one example, could easily have gone over to a phonetic system, no? But those people are far too wise to allow access to just any old body."

"From snow to China. I'm telling you, we've got some really strange types in this organization."

The former professor judged it at about twelve to eighteen degrees Fahrenheit, an untoward temperature for this time of year. It concerned him that the stock of firewood was running low. Relying upon his authority as one of the most senior members, he now summoned the eye doctor and required him, and not for the first time to go outside and collect pine cones for use as kindling.

"I see," the ophthalmologist said with unconscious irony. "First, I have to clean out all those mouse droppings in the flour bin, and now this."

"This is *not*, and I repeat *not*, absinth. I don't care what you fellows claim."

"Sir? Tell us again about all those tricks. The way you've always been able to get hold of so much money? I have to ask."

"*I* don't get hold of it. My money gets hold of it. That's the system." And then: "I told my people to begin arbitraging currency shorts. Going long on interrogation equipment. Took a large position in sorghum futures. And, of course, I'm still shipping arms to Argentina and Brazil. Why work when you have a system like that? After all, if you sincerely want to break a system, you must play along with it at first."

FOURTEEN

For a longtime he had been waiting, the founder, for a tour of the facilities. Had, or had not, his wealth been used in ways to bring a final end to mass democracy? To the reassertion of Caucasian primacy? To the introduction of culture?

"I crave to see the laboratories first of all," said he, reserving the library for "dessert." Suddenly, suffering from his disguise, he pulled off the corrugated rubber "face" he has been constrained to wear. A shout went up. His true appearance was altogether unlike that in FBI posters. Instead of an eighty-one or eighty-two-year-old Hispanic, he looked scarcely more than seventy-eight or seventy-nine.

A very plausible mask modeled after Jose Maria Morelos.

The laboratory was long and narrow commensurate both with the establishment at large and a sizeable number of the members. Dressed in a white laboratory coat and inhalation protectors, he ambled down among the apparatuses, the complex organization of flask and retorts, the jars of anthrax and botulism spores, quantum microscopes of huge expense, and the two bioengineers who had come with them, one from the California Institute of Technology, and the other a community college in occupied Fiji. He shook hands with both these people. Never had he or anyone seen such a collection of reagents, tens of thousands of compounds stored along floor-to-ceiling shelves that ran the length of the already very long room. One could see sulfur compounds of bright yellow together with green substances representing still other salts and minerals and the like.

A cage holding two small rhesus monkeys had been put out of sight in the closet.

"Yes sir, I've never understood it, why ambitious countries go in for nuclear weapons when *so much more* can be done with ordinary bacilli alone."

"And more cheaply, too. Am I right?"

"Absolutely."

"Good. Very good. O.K., I think I'd like to see the library now. That's where the really dangerous stuff is. Shall I wear my nose protectors?"

They moved slowly along the chartreuse corridor, some fifteen geniuses, the book agent, and the provisioner of them all. Last came Karl, the youngest and most uncertain of the whole crew. Really, did he want to grow up and become like one of these?

"Probably," he said, speaking to himself alone.

Nine persons were ranged up and down the reading table, a special sort of people using magnifying glasses and dressed in double-pane glasses. The founder shook hands with all of them, save only one.

"You're holding my life in your hands!" he called out suddenly. "All those books! All those pharmacopeias and farmers' diaries. No one could want a life like yours, not 'less he were as exceptional as me!"

A large applause broke out. A person could scan up and down those half-million volumes, many of them unknown to scholars, and see there the makings of the next revolution, a transplantation of the best people to the moons of Saturn, time travel, parallel universes, holes in time-space, a race of men who wear their trousers around their waists.

He spent almost two hours in that enormous collection, perusing especially seventeenth and eighteenth-century imprints in stalwart bindings with, many of them, marbled endpapers.

The wisdom! The woodcuts! And if he were not himself a super-educated human being, he did know beauty when he saw it.

"Beautiful books!" he said. "I rank them just below music and driving by night 'neath starry skies."

As pertains to driving by night beneath starry skies, this individual was undoubtedly the world's reigning champion.

That was when there came to them the silvery sound of a, naturally, silver bell, which seemed to be calling them to Christmas.

They burst into the room two abreast but then gave way at the last moment to the provider. The tree itself was tall, bathed in purple and violet, and had incunabula dangling from the branches. One would have said, correctly, that there were more than 200 presents either arrayed beneath the tree or hidden in various places. His eye, the founder's, settled upon an oblong gift wrapped in what looked like a page of Anglo-Saxon of about 900 A.D., or soon thereafter. And then, of course, there were the stockings, all of them about to burst from further book-shaped objects in octavo, or twelvemo, or in one case a folio that had burst the seams.

The food must be mentioned as well—partridges in aspic, a compote of oysters from Apalachicola with Swiss chocolate, truffles and other fungi, all of which was not even to mention a five-gallon keg of pale absinth hurriedly fetched all the way from Carthusia by one of the younger people.

"My word," the former professor admitted, "we haven't had a feast like this since… Oh, I don't know. Halloween?"

"Open your presents!" someone yelled at him.

"No, I want to go first." (One of the younger members.)

"You would. No, most of us want to see the expression on Herb's face when he sees what's in store for him."

"I have two people back here who'd be willing to go first."

"Jesus. All right, let Josh go first."

"Yes! That ought to compensate him for his deficiencies."

"What did you say?"

"Deficiencies."

They caught the man before he could do anything. Amazingly, one of the Latinists had already opened his present, doing it *sub-rosa*, so to speak. He held it up for the crowd.

"*A book of Ayres with a triplicitie of musicke*," he cited. "1606."

An especially recherché edition with incorrect page numbering.

"Windet and Browne edition? Great God, I didn't know any copies were left!"

"Good condition, too."

"Very nice. Now if you look over there by the window, you'll see that ole boy with the beard has already gotten into *his* present."

"What is it?"

"What?"

"What *is* it, goddamn it?"

"This? Book. Rather old one, too."

Three men rose and started to go to him, whereupon he opened the thing quickly and recited the title:

"*The sweet thoughts of death and eternity*. Hawkins. Paris. 1632."

"Yi, yi, yi. Give you fifty bucks for it."

"Agreed. I've already got a copy anyway."

"Who's next?"

"*The New Austerities*. Peachtree. 1994."

"Give you a dollar for it."

"*Drole*. I can easily get twice that on the open market. As well you know."

"Next!"

"Victorinus Strigelius. *Part of the harmony of King Dauids harp*. J. Wolfe. 1582."

"The Dexter translation?"

"Lord, no. Where do you get these ideas? Dexter had been dead for seventeen years!"

"Oh, good. He just spilled some of that green liquor all over it."

"Next!"

A tall man arose, a gaunt individual, seldom seen, whose sepulchral face might have served to inspire the monument makers on Easter Island. "*Microcosmographie*," he said. "1628."

"Cosmographie! We can use that."

"Want to sit down, darling? We would appreciate it."

Two hundred and seventeen was the exact number of gifts that were traded back and forth, including the contents of the stockings. One man, it is true, was given a hygiene manual, an insulting gesture that caused him to rise and return to his room. With the absinth only half-finished, the pianist was summoned to play some of the old ballads starting with *Shirleye's Little Boy Childe* which told the fate of a two-months-old English babe afflicted with infantile nostalgia. Once there had been an "England," a devastated area now populated mostly by foreign types.

FIFTEEN

The keg was eventually emptied and when morning came, most of the members were found to be suffering from awful headaches. The linguist was in the infirmary, while the botanist lay unconscious in the purple hall. Himself, the former-professor, wandered in and out among these corpses offering help to those who wanted it. Meanwhile, the founder, once more in Hispanic guise, had gotten into an Egyptian board game of some kind and seemed to be winning.

It was just minutes before 10:00 a.m. when the mathematics boy, an abstracted sort of person burdened with his special ability, drifted into the rectory, coming to a sudden halt when he saw all the adults behaving like drunk persons. The professor caught him.

"Don't look at them," he said, "look at me." And then: "All right look at 'em, if you have to."

Together they hastened to a neutral corner of the enormous room and after taking possession of a red leather couch, the professor's favorite, began to make comments about the members.

"Look at that one. He's probably the second finest biotechnologist in the whole world, but, oh my goodness, look at the face on him."

"Yeah. He looks like a…"

Only the horticulturist was a better-than-average-looking man.

"Yes. But why oh why can't the best people also look the best? Makes me mad."

"Well, I…"

"You going to drink that coffee? Or just stare at your reflection?"

The boy drank.

"And over there. That one has sexual proclivities."

"I know! He was the one who..."

"Never mind about that. What I want to talk about is this: how is it, Karl, that people can be only just so good, and not one bit better? Why shouldn't we be able to progress eternally, and then keep on going? This is a problem that affects me particularly."

"Well..."

"Precisely. I tell you this, that someday we're going to collide into a race of people who *can* go on forever, wiser and wiser, possessed of perfect integrity, enclosed in forms as gorgeous as their souls."

"Wow. Awesome."

"The moons of Uranus. Or more likely in *Proxima Centuri*—that's where we'll find 'em. Oh, I see—you expect them to be hostile, yes?"

He could hardly have been more mistaken as to their true location.

"Maybe."

"Drink up! Listen my boy, they *should* be hostile, when they see what we are. I would encourage them to deal with us as we dealt with the Neanderthals. And as we *should have* dealt with certain others."

"Yeah, but ...!"

"*Racism*, that's what I recommend. It has been the default philosophy of 99% of humanity over 99% of life on earth. Can 50 billion people have been so wrong?"

"Oh boy. There you go."

"Racism is how the Neanderthal mostly—I don't say completely—disappeared. Think we'd have biotechnology if racists hadn't done their bit? Opera? Mahler? My boy, I can accept anything so long as it opposes equality."

He allowed the genius a plate of eggs and sausage, toast, coffee, and several other good-smelling things that brought the professor around to asking for the same.

"A true person," he said, "wouldn't have any use for food. Nor oxygen neither. These are simply weaknesses, you understand, that bind us to the material world. When I hear about human 'pleasures,' that's when I draw my gun. Truth is, there's only one real source of pleasure — and I know you won't believe this — one real source that's available only to people… Well, to people like me, to be absolutely honest about it. Drink up."

"Like you?"

"Yes. And like Howard Peevy over there. See him? He can go four days without food and writes some of the eeriest poetry ever heard. O.K., this is how it works: you want pleasure, you must first put yourself in touch with the supernal. You don't believe that, of course. Go mono-a-mono with the transcendental. I know a singer who studied for thirty years but was never allowed on stage. Why would she do that? We have here among us a Greek grammarian whose father studied under Denniston. Could never earn a living in the outside world."

The Greek Particles (1934).

"Not good."

"These are the ones we care about, me and you, those who will trade thirty years for just one peep at the other world."

"Whew! Must really be something. Well, I need to go get some firewood now, and…"

"Hold it right there! You're worse than Alcibiades. Too soft are you to join with us and seek the ineffable? Perhaps you really don't belong in this place."

A comment the ex-professor would eventually retract.

They had more coffee, too much really, and then began to assist some of the more helpless members back to their apartments. Especially, they helped a man whose name was called after a certain cartoon character and who had recently been given charge of the institution's radio telescope array. His apartment was not at all as tidy as it ought to have been and seemed to conflict with his known character, which had always been notoriously well-organized. The ex-professor noticed at once that he had brought several large cardboard boxes into his bedroom, and that one of them was spilling over with clothes and books and bits and pieces of pipe cleaning equipment.

"I think you could use some coffee Goofy. Here, I'll fix some for you."

"I do not need coffee, and I'm not drunk. I have not been drunk in years, and I want no part of that noxious beverage you people are always promoting."

"I see. But still, you don't look quite right, if I may say so."

"I have not been right in years. I *am* flattered however that you've noticed at last."

"Well good gracious, why haven't you spoken up? We have pills for that. And a really good counselor who has helped lots of us. He even helped me last year, and if he can help me, he can help anybody!" He chortled, chortling alone.

"Remember, Herb, when you said that people like us are the unacknowledged legislators of the world?"

"I do. I stole that from some long-ago poet of course, and changed it all about."

"And this legislation, has it done us any good?"

"Well! Not yet, I guess."

"And Herb?"

"Yes?"

"I can hardly see you in all this lantern light."

He turned up the light, the professor, and waited to see what further confessions were likely to be forthcoming from his intermittent friend. "I notice," he said, "that you've been putting things in that cardboard box."

"Herb?"

"Yes?"

"Maybe it never gets better because it just can't. Maybe it's the nature of things. And maybe we aren't getting better either!"

"Lots of people would agree with that."

"And Herb?"

"Yes?"

"If it never gets better, then maybe...."

"O.K., I see where you're going. Stop it."

"Never gets better, then maybe..."

"Didn't I just tell you to stop? What if the founder heard what you're fixing to say?"

"Maybe we ought never have evolved in the first place."

"Me, too, I've wondered about that, too," the young mathematician contributed.

"This is how I see it." (He had gotten up off the floor, had Goofy, and had taken up a position with his accustomed rigidity in a straight back chair.) "A man is walking down a country road, right? He espies a heap of gold on one side and a stack of manure on the other."

"And?"

"And so why does he prefer the manure? Why does he patronize hockey games and watch the seepage on television? And why does our constitution cater to such people?"

"It were better in Medieval China, is that what you think?"

"Why no, and that's just the point. It never was and never will be any better than, say, a 'four' on civilization's ten-scale."

"He's right," the youngest of them said.

"Shut up. Didn't I see you, Goof, just two days ago ecstasizing over your newest project? And hasn't Jones shelled out sixteen million on equipment just for you? And haven't you been awarded six hours a month at the quantum telescope on Mt. Fabius?"

This project represented an effort to synthesize solar sails of frozen hydrogen . Just one atom in gross thickness, the sails would have possessed almost no weight at all, and would have "accelerated," (no pun intended) the achievement of light speed by intergalactic sailing vessels.

"I suppose. But how about all those other hours in the month? Not worth it, Herb. In my whole life, I've had maybe two dozen of those hours you keep talking about. The rest has been all eating and sleeping and pissing. Where's the dignity in that, Herb?"

"I haven't even had *one* hour yet," the youth admitted.

"Oh for God's sakes. I'm going to tell Jones what you said! O.K., I won't tell him. But I'm getting thoroughly unhappy with you, my man. *Thoroughly*!"

Working cooperatively, the youth and professor came forward from each's prior location, approached the depressive, lifted him (who seemed actually to be amused by all this) and arranged him, suit and all, in his four-post bed with carvings on the headboard.

SIXTEEN

The old-time professor and his young colleague hastened on down to the red and gold intersection, shook hands briefly and then parted ways, one to go in one direction and the other another. Both these persons were deserving of literary scrutiny, but the professor was far the more interesting type. Always thinking, *that* was his bad habit. Anyone seeing him from a distance of say thirty or forty feet, might say he had a toothache, or that he'd been born that way, or had uncovered truths too awful to share. At times like these, he might hurry home again, get undressed, and take shelter in the rich white bosoms of his understanding wife.

He was already halfway to his wife when he bounced up against yet another scientist, a phthisic Lithuanian devoted to "out of the body" experiments. He had, perhaps, left his body once too often, this person, to judge from the horror-eyed expression that had become permanent with him. Today he carried a slice of toast in his hand, most of it gone. They bowed to each other, the scientist bowing slightly more.

A few random crumbs had lodged in his somewhat obscene-looking moustache.

"Herb?"

"Dwayne! Still suffering from your hangover?"

"Lord no. I have ways to deal with that."

"A way to escape, is that what it is?" He laughed. "I've always envied you that."

"You seen the founder?"

"Not lately. Why?"

"Couple of federal people been nosing about. Tall one and short one."

"Oh, good; I know that short one. He's actually more loathsome than that Interior Department guy."

"Hate to hear that!"

"Maybe we can get away by jumping out of our bodies, eh what? Doing somersaults in the air? Ha! Ha!"

"Laugh, do. I'm here to tell you that my way is the only way. The only way to get to our future home in other universes."

"Again with that?"

"There's only one thing, Herb, that's faster than Goofy's solar sails, and that's thought itself."

"You've been thinking? You need to be more careful about that."

"Listen to me: a man can go to the edge of the cosmos and back again on wings of thought alone. I'm doing it right now."

"Need some coffee?"

"Certainly. That would be second-best only to a daiquiri made with vodka."

They retreated into the professor's apartment, an ornamented sanctuary with framed documents, books of course, a terrarium, a fish bowl with just one specimen in it, and a middle-aged wife with deep rich breasts.

"A seven-room apartment you've got here Herb but apparently not a single drop of vodka."

They sat, both of them fixated on the procedures of a large yellow lizard running back and forth through the obstacles of a glass-enclosed Ordovician landscape assembled by the professor's wife.

"A home on other planets. There's something very inviting about that Dwayne. What sort of society do you propose for such a place?"

"I knew you'd ask." (He still had a tad of toast left over, a fragment of not greatly more than two square inches or less. Unfortunately, a blob of margarine had fallen onto the carpet where the man was trying in vain to hide it beneath a shoe that was so flat and wide that it filled the distance between the two men.) "What sort of society? A totalitarian society under the rule of a tiny number of race-conscious, Caucasian geniuses presiding over an aesthetocracy free of humanitarian conceits."

Even in the rarified precincts of the organization he had been reluctant to expose his views.

"This is why we get along so well, you and me."

"Beauty is superior to science after all, and harder to instantiate. Superior even to those who create it."

They had not always gotten along so well.

"How so?"

"Because it participates in transcendency. And gives advance glimpses of what people like me and maybe even you can expect."

"I can expect to be like you?"

"Oh, not really. But you're all right in some ways."

They drank further coffee mixed, if not with vodka, with Puerto Rican rum at any rate. The woman was attentive, or pretended to be, and was supplying the sort of rapt attention both these man required in audiences of theirs.

"Beauty," the physicist continued, "would be just as beautiful even if humans had never existed. That's because beauty is a real thing and not merely an opinion."

"You're out of step with post-modern opinion. I may be the last living person in the world disposed to agree with you."

"Clear blue lakes, Herb, on the black side of the sun."

"Yes. And I'll raise you mile-high waves that break into billions of splinters as they come to land."

"You're good at this, Herb. Better than I expected."

"While as for the seas on other planets, I think of them as tenuous, as blue, and as lucid as air. But reverting back to what you said earlier; there *is* no black side to the sun, we both know that."

That was when the lamp, having exhausted the daily kerosene ration, sputtered off while leaving the corridor in an almost complete darkness with dogs and intellectuals roaming back and forth. One man had a candle, another a cigarette that glowed more and more brightly the further he sucked on it. In the distance two of the members had abandoned their rooms and were debating vehemently about something or another. The professor was about to retire to his own place and to the cited breasts of his woman when at that moment the man known as Alphonse (a pseudonym) strolled up looking for a quarrel. A Byzantinist, only about 5'4" in total height, he sincerely believed he had the best head in the whole institution. Dwayne refused to look at him.

"Is this an interesting discussion?" he asked. "Or should I continue on my way?"

"No, no. We were just talking about time and space, life and beauty, stuff like that."

"Hey, those are *my* specialties!"

"And current conditions."

"Conditions?"

"Why, yes. How long has it actually been since you were in the outside world, Al? It's dreadful out there!"

Despite his general aggressiveness, the man was terrified of the outside world and had visited there only once in the preceding twelve years.

"So I've heard. No really, I think you gentlemen are making a great mistake by giving attention to such things. Surely you must know by now what humans are."

"And yet there *are* some of us who still believe..."

In actuality, none of them truly believed any such thing.

"Who believe we can do good deeds and make discoveries?" (He broke suddenly into a hoarse laughter that must have traveled the whole length of the hall, judging from the size of his voice.)

"You laugh," the-out-of-the-body man observed. "I knew you would."

"I knew, too. It has to do with 'averaging,' you understand. The 'averaging' that necessarily takes place when ordinary types come together. Society simply cannot endure people like you and me. It demoralizes them and hurts their feelings. There's some evidence that it might even impact the gross national... gross domestic product!"

In the whole group, not a single one of them qualified for an economist.

"Even so, there really are some things that are good for all of us."

"Such as enough to eat? Good habitation and social esteem? Freedom from disease? Health giving vaccinations and sex in all its permutations? 360-degree television sets? People on the northern shore of Long Island have all of these and more. And have you visited there recently?"

Also prestigious educational degrees for the masses, affirmative burials, low cost escrubilators, etc.

SEVENTEEN

Time, continuing perfunctorily, brought further darkness both by night and day alike. It was obvious by now that the source of their electricity had been taken from them, a punishment, as it were, for being the people they were. And then, too, there was the case of the geologist who had gone for kerosene and never come back again.

Looking for controversy, Alphonse had wandered down to the great room and was spending a few minutes in front of the fire. He had received a three-day-old newspaper in the mails and was impatient to discuss it with his colleagues. Starting with the most prominent news, he spoke out loud and clear, rousing some of the members from their naps.

"Listen to this," he said. "Silly Logan" (rock singer) "is divorcing Marcus" (basketball player) "Whimple!"

"Oh dear."

"And look here, she's asking twelve million, but wants Marcus to take the children."

"A person could buy a lot of books with twelve million. Wait a minute, isn't she the one that gave the Vice-President a blow job?"

But Alphonse kept on reading. "Hmmm," he said, "appears that we killed 127 terrorists just last Wednesday alone. Never knew what hit 'em."

"Terrorists?"

"They're always terrorists, if killed by us." (He divided the paper into pages, giving the members one sheet each.)

"Chicago basketball team is .552 on the season. Hey, maybe we should subscribe to this paper."

"Oh, oh. Seems that an African American youth was offended last week in Oklahoma. They're sending a team of therapists."

"Hey! Aluminum was up last week!"

"Good."

"But expendables were down."

"Yes, and I was on the wrong side," mournfully said the founder.

Much to the contrary, Congress in joint session had ceded seven Pacific islands to the brave little state.

"Says here that the Israeli cabinet has absolutely refused even to consider giving us that refund."

"Get lots of books with that kind of money."

"Says here that Nebraska has been cited for a disproportionate number of same-race marriages. The governor has apologized."

"Gentlemen! New York is opening two more transgendering boutiques. Overcrowding. Almost caused a riot."

"Well, at least they've finally mandated insurance coverage for those people. *Retro*gendering, too."

"Twenty million allocated for tattoo erasure."

"Say, if they can transgender people, d'you think they could turn me into an eagle? A real big one?"

"Hmm. They're giving early release to black prisoners in San Fernando. They need the space."

"Oh gosh; Farrar Straus has folded. They were the last of those people."

"Always wanted to be an eagle."

Very doubtful that he knew anything about the usual tribulations of these birds.

"Have you seen these figures for the national debt?" (He held up the sheet for all to see.)

"Laugh, if you must, but not everything is bad. A laboratory in San Diego has finally come up with an antidote to penile extenders."

These words were followed by a unanimous sort of laughter that engulfed the room and caused the chandelier to chime.

EIGHTEEN

In their desire to become yet more sequestered than they were, they made every feasible effort to avoid the state, federal, county, and European Union inspectors who had taken over one of the apartments and were on the search, they said, of fire code violations. And then in January, the adjudicator appointed the insane person, the sole member to have earned their respect, to serve in a liaison capacity with the mentioned officials. These four could often be seen at the back of the yellow corridor sampling various drugs taken from fire code violators in this and neighboring townships. But it wasn't until February 19th that the preceptor, poorly disguised, was identified and chased down, forced into a corner and made to answer questions.

"Well lookie here," the state agent said. "Got us a big fish this time. I don't know, sir, but sometimes I think you've been trying to avoid us!"

"Yeah, got us a big fish," the county agent said. "And he's been trying to avoid us, too!"

Not dismayed, the superintendent looked back at them coolly. And yet his voice, when finally he used it, proved weak and seemed to come from far away:

"We don't allow illegal substances in this building."

"Don't?"

"Or very rarely anyway. For those who need it. Or the very old. No, we're a law abiding bunch, most of us, and have full respect for government at all its levels."

"'Law abiding,' he says. 'Full respect for the law.' Har! Har Whee! All right, so why don't you bring out your minority people, hm? So's we can look at 'em."

The conversation now devolved onto the federal man, far the heaviest, tallest, best-paid, and most ignorant human being ever to have come this deep into the building. His tie, displaying the 56-state flag, gave evidence of the foods he had spilled, while as for the man's head, it looked as if it had been formed by an exasperated sculptor who had lost interest in the project. It looked like a boulder without features, or like a brown potato with only the least indications of a nose or mouth. It looked like an artifact recovered from the ancient Near East, or like a bowling ball with holes in place of sensory equipment, or like a November pumpkin that had been kicked back and forth by wild children. It looked like the face of a manatee staring back from the bottom of the sea.

It looked like a number of other things, as well, and contrasted unfavorably with the state inspector's, a smaller sort of man who stood just an inch or two on the wrong side of normality. This might almost have been a handsome person, had not his two matched nostrils been three times larger than his eyes. He would have preferred, the adjudicator, to deal with this person; instead, the federal man forced him with two strong arms to look into his eyes only.

We have never claimed that mere normality ought to set the standard for good looks. Nor race, gender, orientation, I.Q., national origin, nor anything else either.

"Look, 'buddy,' I want to see some niggers and queers in this here outfit. And I don't give a good goddamn how many colleges you went to!"

"Yes, well we're looking into that. Next time you come, we'll have more negroes than you can shake a stick at!"

"That's what you said last time!"

"Ja, that's what you say last time!" the German pointed out. Suddenly, he stepped forward and aimed a kick at the supervisor, missing by little.

Feeling quite helpless, the rector turned then to the county man, a wee little person backed up solely by the rather meager resources of a district recently fallen into debt. The federal man, by contrast, had nuclear weapons.

"No, I do want to be helpful," said the supervisor, speaking into the ear of the county inspector, the only one who might be persuadable. "How many negroes do we need actually?"

"Huh?"

"How many?"

"Yeah, right. Huh?"

The superintendent returned to the original man. "You knew that we already have a Lithuanian?"

"Yeah? I doubt it. O.K., bring her on out here so's we can look at her."

"Let me see if I can find him."

"Hold it! Just hold it right there; you ain't going nowhere. What, you think I'm *stoopid* or something?"

"Stu...! How on earth could you be stupid and work for the Federal Government? I mean! It's not as if there's affirmative action for your kind."

"You're right about that."

"It's people like me that need affirmative action."

"I've seen worse."

They debated until just past 4:00, at which moment the superintendent took advantage of a lull in the conversation and managed to escape through the squash court. By hap, three Vietnamese visitors were being entertained in the tea room, and the supervisor

Two were Japanese actually. It was the Vietnamese woman who gave the orders however. Or, they might all be Koreans.

was able to take a place among them without bringing much notice to himself. The guests had been meditating a retreat like this for themselves, a place of sanctuary against certain imperial mandates now bearing down upon them. In return they had promised to take as many as 50 legal and illegal immigrants back to where they belonged.

"Many books," one of them said, an ochre-colored man with an intelligent aspect. So intelligent, indeed, that it was difficult to see how he had managed to get past customs. "You have many books!"

"Yes."

"And make revolution, no? Book make revolution?"

"Ha! Revolution. But who can say what might happen? You get a couple of books into a couple of the right kind of hands..."

"Pearl Harbor!"

They laughed, all. A Pearl Harbor of the mind, shoot yes. That was when the heaviest, tallest, best-paid, and most intelligent-looking of the three men rose from his place, took a wrapped package from under his chair and passed it over to the preceptor. Could anything have been more appreciated than a few old volumes of Japanese or Korean literature inscribed on rice paper? Woodblock impressions? Rarities possessed by no other sanctuary on earth? With his hand trembling visibly, the supervisor opened the package and drew out a most delicate looking codex on rice paper. He turned right away to the first of the great many woodblock engravings and then, glancing up at the primary Japanese, waited to hear what he already half-expected:

"Only copy."

There were five white men in that crowd, and at least two of them seemed near to fainting.

Not strictly true. Two further copies were later on discovered among the possessions of the county official.

"The only goddamned copy in the whole goddamn world! That's what he said. Said it's the only goddamned copy in the world!"

"And you believe him?"

"He comes to our country, drinks our tea, and then hands over his country's last remaining copy! We need more like him. Lots more."

"Right, yeah. But what are we going to give him in return?"

The nine people quickly finished off their tea and then stood up as a unit and proceeded straightway to the gallery that ran down the whole length of the chartreuse hall. By no means was this a major art collection; it did however include a good many expert copies and even a few originals representing the more important movements since late Roman times. It formed a goodly sight, all the way down to 1919, at which point the selection pretty much came to a stop. They were left admiring, or rather not admiring, a piece of modernistic garbage posted there to give a date to the moment Western Civilization also began to turn to garbage.

It is of course true that contemporary historians cite different dates for the inception of Western decay. Those most commonly mentioned are: 1919, 1871, 1848, and 1281.

"Let's give him that one," mooted Sylvester Brody, a rascally sort of person who was fond, too fond really, of practical jokes. When he grinned, his nose went red and his enormous teeth filled the horizon. And yet he had many good friends among the membership. Stepping forward, he put on a solemn face much like those of the three Vietnamese.

Many? Hardly. He had the same number of friendships as his friend, who also had just one.

"Honored sirs," he said, "I want to offer you this little example of my country's respect for yours. See that splotch in the middle? It represents all sorts of metaphysical representations, too many to list really. Heck, you could get millions for this" — (this was true) — "on the New York market! Makes me sick even to think of giving it up. But... It is what it is. What can I say? Here's looking at you."

NINETEEN

And now the days went past two and three at a time, as it seemed to some of the more innumerate types. But when at last Saturday came around, the members put aside their Korean and Japanese grammars and went outside. Dismayed to find the chicken house covered with snow, they ran for shovels and set to work. It proved an arduous project that yielded up some eight or nine colored eggs left over from one of their scrupulously-observed holidays. Frozen hard as stones, they held out small promise of nutritional value. (The fowls had died of exposure some two or three days earlier and were given over to the dogs.) By this time it was past 2:46 p.m. The wind was severe, the snow continuing, and the sun in dark phase.

"What's the use," the geologist called, "of trying to do anything in this weather? Let's go inside."

They ran for it, which is to say until the superintendent had formed them up in single file. It was 3:02 by now, and this most crepuscular of all afternoons already looked like night. And that was the moment, while they were furnishing themselves with coffee and cider, that the carpenter suddenly remembered it was just minutes before the physicist was scheduled to come awake from his long sleep.

"Almost time!" he shouted.

The people harkened to him and came running. Truth was, the membership was simply unwilling to let so brilliant a scientist carry through with destroying himself, wherefore they had entered his apartment late at night and had injected him with a dormancy agent calibrated to remain effective for three weeks and two days, exactly. Each man now came forward in rotation and, bending over the sleeper's face, tried to imagine what he had been dreaming about during that time.

"What a strange expression!"

"I wouldn't talk about peoples' faces. If I were you."

"He's been to hell and back! Or maybe paradise."

"Watch it! Don't knock over that intravenous stuff for Christ's sakes."

"Hey, that's a REM sleep he's got going there, palpably so!"

The founder came forward, the crowd making way for him. "I've seen that expression before," he said, "if I remember rightly. In Nepal, I believe."

The theory that this was indeed a REM sleep appeared to have been validated by the sleeping member's member, suffering from tumescence.

"Good Lord."

"Ignore it. It's entirely natural under the circumstances."

"I thought I saw his eye blink!"

"Which one?"

"Which one? That seems important to you, does it? He's got two. One of them blinked. And?"

"We'll have to throw the mattress away. Three weeks worth of bodily waste. I don't like things like that."

"Now it's the other eye. Hell, he's already about thirty seconds late."

They waited impatiently, waiting right up until both eyes opened at once and the man yawned and stretched and got up and began pulling on his clothes.

"He doesn't even know we're here!"

"Or doesn't care. God, what a mess. Give him another injection, O.K.?"

That was when the physicist turned and threw up both hands, astonished to find some twenty or more geniuses crammed into his average-size apartment. "What's the story?" he asked. "Have I been snoring?"

It needed better than an hour to bring the man back to reality, throw him under the shower, and then refresh him with coffee and high content apple cider. Even then he continued to look all about in "wild surmise," as that previously-quoted poet had preemptively described him.

"Good to have you back," someone said. "You've slept enough to last for years!"

"But look at the expression on his face."

"Yes. Very odd," the eye doctor said.

"No, that's just a temporary symptom, that expression, and will eventually fade away."

"We hope."

"Remember, we don't know what happened to him during all that time. Bad dreams, water in the lungs, incontinence. It could be anything."

"We know about the incontinence part."

The awakened man now spoke up. He had been sitting on the edge of the bed playing with his fingers while looking down at the floor. "Bad dreams," he said.

The crowd moved in closer.

"But I can't remember what they were."

"Ach! What a pity. I expect your bad dreams were much more interesting than most peoples'."

"That's not necessary. Not at all. For example, in *my* case..."

"We can talk about your case later on, Harold. Just now we need to hear what this fellow has to say."

↑ These lines are self-explanatory. ↓

Harold snorted, suddenly arose, and then exited by the left-side door.

"Hypnotize him."

Who said that?"

"Why, yes. Hypnotize him and make him spill the beans!"

"We are most definitely *not* going to make him do anything he doesn't want! Repeat: *not*." (This pronouncement was followed by a two-minute silence.) "Unless he wants us to.

"Want to, Hans? Want us to make you? Want us to put you to sleep again so you can tell us about it? What d'you say, hm? You don't have to of course, but do you *want* to?"

"For informational reasons only. Think how valuable that could be! And besides, we won't tell."

"Don't greatly care what you do," the awakened man confessed.

"You hear that? If he's going to insist on it, we need to honor that, I think. Go get Clarence."

A psychologist, hypnotist, beer can collector, graphologist, and all-round pain-in-the-ass, this *Clarence* was, perhaps, the most experienced hypnotist in the entire organization. Only once had he been known to betray a confidence, a piece of misbehavior that had earned him some two-thirds of a million dollars. Dressed in a satin robe, he entered the apartment in high dignity, proceeded straightway to the kitchen and retrieved a can of beer from the refrigerator. Finally, coming eye-to-eye with the subject, he whispered a few words and then drew a rabbit's foot from his vest and held it up where the physicist could see it. Some few seconds went by, which is to say, until the entranced man began speaking rapidly in a language no one understood.

"O.K., what the hell is that?"

"Noise. He's simply making noises."

"I don't think so! No, it has that lilt to it of an Indo-European language."

They continued to listen, right up until the distraught man began actually yelling out loud in his strange idiom.

"Just hear those clusters! It doesn't seem possible, how he sticks half a dozen consonants all together in one big mess!"

"This is a *Slavic* language my friends, no slightest doubt."

"He's right," said the eye doctor, the organization's sole monolingual man.

"Where's old Stavros? Now that we need him."

He was fetched, this Stavros, from the fourth cell counting backwards along the lilac corridor. A grumpy individual known to have personally slaughtered at least two persons while living in post-Soviet Hungary, he entered the room, halted, and looked about slowly at each individual person.

"So!" he said. "You need old Stavros after all!"

An intimidating individual.

"We've always needed you! Sometimes."

"Besides, you're the only one who understands Russian."

"This not Russian what he say."

"Croatian then?"

"What!"

"Sorry."

"Czech people," he said. "They talk this."

"Well, of course!" They slapped themselves punitively on their foreheads. One man slapped his knee. "No doubt this is the poor fellow's default language. Or one of them anyway."

"Can you translate it?"

"What!"

"Sorry."

He was given pad and pen and invited to use the desk. The noises were coming more speedily now, so much so, indeed, that large numbers of them had coalesced into nothing more than a train of uninterrupted consonants that to an innocent ear sounded like a sequence of some of the worst parts of German or Finnish. And all this time he was writing as fast as he could, the translator, losing much of it in the radio-like static that came from the hypnotized man. Arriving from a distant part of the room, the young mathematician attempted to see what was being written.

"Hey, that's not English!" he said, addressing the room at large.

"Thanks for that bit of information. I suppose he can write in whatever language he wants, no? Especially since he isn't being paid."

"What!"

The process went on for a solid fifteen or twenty minutes, until the subject gave signs of changing over from his hypnotized state into outright sleep.

"He hasn't had enough sleep; he wants more."

"Shut up, Lester!"

"Tell you what, Stavros, you put that script into English for us, and you can have my dessert tonight."

Being the person that he was, (overweight by a good forty pounds), the Slav readily agreed to that. The syndics never imagined that it would absorb more than three days for what ought to have been a fifteen-minute job.

Follows here a crude version with numerous interruptions of the very imperfect English redaction of the original Czech.

> Felt that I was falling, falling through light years of [static][interruption] tall red building [interruption] coming in and out. Beyond doubt a city of some kind, [static] crowded, with mile-high towers looking [static] a quarantined landscape [static] cattle as small as cats. No white people anywhere. I felt [long interruption] staring at me. Never in my life [interruption] such poverty, such awful behavior, [interruption] urinating in streets, facial scars, naked [interruption] [brief static] Couldn't believe it. [interruption] standing on the corner. 'Motherfu [static] hole!' he said. 'You better git yore [interruption] here!' [Long interruption] [static] [fade out] cock-sucking son [interruption] Dow industrials. Technologies [interruption] supporting actress.

A conscientious rendering validated by experts.

It was a most fragmentary excerpt, to be sure and had required the translator to fill in some of the blanks by guesswork or by analogy with phrases often seen in post-modern fiction. It recalled to the ex-professor's mind the year he had devoted to a just-then-discovered slip of papyrus of Theopompos of some 170 words. Or those two years he had spent with a large New York publisher separating dreck from the unprofitable stuff.

"Well!" he said. "Gives a fairly dismal picture, doesn't it, of what we may look forward to! Assuming it's at all accurate."

"Oh, it's accurate all right. Been outside lately?"

The mood was negative enough, the geniuses and near-geniuses looking about at each other in, to repeat, "wild surmise." Wasn't that enough? No, for this was the exact instant that the three inspectors (supported by half a dozen others) broke into the room, demanding DNA specimens from each and every one.

TWENTY

This time the infraction had to do with the organization's unacceptable, social impact report.

"You sit here," the town inspector said. "You don't vote, you don't talk to people, and yet we have the best goddamn basketball team in the state!"

"Just too busy, I guess. Sorry about that," the supervisor said.

"And what's the deal with that one? Damn!"

"He's asleep."

"I know he's asleep! Hell, I probably knew it before you did. Wake him up! Unless you want me to stick this here swab up his nose."

In the event, the man's nose yielded a pale green sort of DNA that went direct into a test tube with a cork in it. The others yielded passively to the procedure, all save Stavros, who had a warrant on him from the European Community. Insofar as was known, the social-impact-people hadn't yet seen the library or even knew that it existed. To turn their attention in another direction, the group's prime cellist, an astringent sort of fellow with big ears, offered to conduct them to breakfast, a pleasing invitation that was accepted.

The following two days passed without major interruption. The young, mathematics genius was always in his cell, always scribbling, always hoping to solve a certain infamous conundrum that for two hundred years had baffled the educated world. And, in fact, he actually did receive honorable mention in one of the journals emitted by the Haitian Institute of

Technology. He grew a beard. He no longer looked like his actual 22 years; he looked 23.

The most spiritually inclined of the members was the previously-mentioned former professor who had been discharged from two leading universities. These days he spent with his wife, an old style sort of woman with a notable figure and unstinted dedication to her man. They used to lie next to each other, whispering memories into each other's ear. In recent weeks, Sanskrit had become his hobby, a pursuit that had carried him deep into some of the very deepest part of the Hindu wisdom. He had his peculiarities to be sure, chief among them that he made no distinction between his own personal interests and those of civilization in general, and that he comprised the organization's leading spokesman for the view that high art was the conduit to eternity.

A divinity in human form, who is known to have seen this description.

To consider the ophthalmologist next, these past few months had been a strain on him. Lacking any sort of clear-cut genius, he had striven to close the gap in terms of the books he had read, the science and music and the rest. On the other hand, he had greatly assuaged the difficulties some of these old people were having with their vision. Here, behind these walls, his former wife could have no hope of finding him.

The one-armed man now spent his time either walking in the woods, or hunting pheasants, or engrossed in sexual congress with his woman. Annoyed that her application for membership had been declined, he gave mounting evidence that he might leave the place in days to come. And then, too, he had proved to be significantly more ignorant than previously understood.

By contrast, the cellist, only recently admitted, formed a major asset for the corporation. For example, he might be called to the supervisor's office late at night to perform the cello concerto of Shostakovich, or one of his own adaptations of Debussy or Ravel. A cheerful man, normally, he was capable of idiosyncratic behavior, of speaking in his sleep and gazing for long periods into the exceptional views that compassed the building on three sides. He had a golden cigarette case containing a small blue lizard victualed on injured flies.

The Slavic man, called Stavros, was engaged full time in his history of Hungarian affairs in the period between the two world wars.

The more he went on with it the more vehement his writings and his behavior at mess, in the bowling lane and tennis courts. Silent at table, he consumed quantities of all kinds of meat with beer and black bread.

In the matter of prestige, it was of course the book agent who outranked nearly everyone. He had frequented so many book fairs, so many auctions (sometimes in disguise), and had taken ownership of so many sought-for volumes that a movement had been put afoot to snatch away his passport. He could sniff out precious books in the haylofts of Picardy, in the recesses of antique furniture stores, at the Vatican and in Bucharest. He had disadvantaged the Lilly Library in Bloomington, Indiana with his thefts and had brought back the best collection of Singhalese writings on deposit in the West. For these and other reasons, he had a permanent reservation at the best place in the refectory whence he could view at leisure the fog-cloaked valley with its red barns and tiny little farmers athwart their machines and animals.

A small bronze plate memorializes the spot.

Very little has yet been revealed about the billionaire who made everything possible. A gifted youth growing up in Massachusetts, he had learned at

It was at this point in the narrative that the author of these glosses, Dr. Brent Wainsford, Ph.D, passed away on June 9.

an early age about the egalitarianism approach to life and its effects upon the human soul. Wanting to protect himself from people of that kind, he had transferred to Texas when he was nineteen and had set to work taking care of cattle, waitering in a restaurant and attending night classes at the enormous university in Austin. But the rest you know, how he did one thing and another, ending up in imports and exports and vending weapons to right-wing governments in Latin America. It is true that he hadn't accrued his first million dollars until fairly late in life (as compared to other people of his type), when finally, he had contracted an open marriage with a woman congruent with his ambitions. Thereafter, his fortune began to develop "of itself," as writers like to say with regard to their own projects.

Eventually he turned into an old man, only 5'2" tall, condemned to drift forever between countries that lacked extradition treaties. Thus far, he had evaded the enforcement arms of the SEC, the FBI, the SPLC, and the western branch of the Diversity Department housed in Santa Fé. Truth was, he had surfeited himself on the pleasures of great wealth, up to and beyond the saturation point, and had determined to use the rest of his time and fortune revenging himself upon those who had demanded that all things be equal, whether horses and books, restaurants and political systems, or cars and human races.

Ends here a brief catalog of the character and quiddities of some of the story's featured people.

TWENTY-ONE

Danger for the founder, who might be identified at any time. In that case, he would certainly be taken to Washington, his fortune seized and collated and added to the off-line appropriation for the recruitment of immigrants. (Emboldened by the last election, the government had quickly begun to move toward a more comprehensive solution of the Caucasian problem.) Men with telescopes had been seen pacing back and forth along the mountain ridges.

They entered the founder's suite, the four men elected to the task, at just past 3:00 in the morning and, after rousing the founder, appareled him in such a way — blue jeans, open shirt, earring, two piercings — that he could more easily mix with normal people. From a distance of about thirty feet, he looked more or less like a superannuated party guy who had grown old while standing out in the middle of a dance floor. More precisely, he looked like a Mestizo with a decent tincture of European in him or rather like a darker-than-usual Chinese free of that peculiarity associated with those peoples' eyes. With his stoop and clothes, he also looked like one or another of certain other sorts of people, a Peruvian, for example, or an old-time cowboy in jeans and open shirt.

For luggage, he was allowed nothing beyond what he could carry in his pockets, and even then he was made to leave his tobacco plug behind. Two cups of hot coffee were decanted into his maw, a surprisingly large cavity filled with diamond implants that sparkled in the light of the flashlight. Finally, he was encouraged to take two slices of toast, one of them deeply appointed with quince jelly and the other quite bare. It was at this point, or slightly later, that he began to regain consciousness and pay some attention to the danger on all sides.

"All I ever wanted was to serve humanity," he said, not without some self pity in his elderly voice. "And do good for all persons everywhere, regardless of race, orientation, class, gender, and sexual selection!" (He had a four-day-old copy of *The New York Times* under one arm.) "Where are we actually?"

He was ushered through the metal detector and then hustled out into the cold. The moon was in dreadful condition and the topmost layer of snow seemed to be migrating *against* the grain of the wind. That was when the benefactor, imperiled by his own slight weight, began to be genuinely troubled by the wild currents of wind. Quickly, they dusted him off, pointed him in the right direction and prodded him in a southwesterly direction where, hopefully, a 1997 Lincoln Town Car waited to receive him.

But didn't get far before they were brought to a halt by a tall man with a rifle. The gun had a telescope on it with a broken lens that reflected a discontinuous image of the stars and moon. The founder picked up speaking once again:

"All people everywhere, and I don't give a rat's ass about national preference and stuff like that. My own wife was from Jersey for Christ's sakes!"

The rifleman greeted him in kindly fashion. "Going for a little stroll are we? At 3:14 in the morning? LOL."

"Couldn't sleep."

The man laughed. He wore a leather jacket and had a badge inscribed in Latin.

"Well!" he said. "Let's make this short. And then you can be on your way! How many tobacco smokers would you say are holed up over in that building"—he pointed to it with his rifle—"holed up over there?"

"None. Not any. Well, we do have one fellow using camphor compresses. But that's all."

"Did I ask about compresses? I don't think so. No, I think I was asking about tobacco. T O B A C C O. Got it?" And then: "We know about them books, too."

The member went pale, so much so that his face lost all contrast against the snow. One man tried to run.

"All you hoity-toity people. Your day is ending, didn't you know that? *Gotterdammerung*, right?"

"Right. Everybody knows how this story will end."

"You got that right! You can push people only so far. O.K., what the hell, I'm going to let you through this time."

They formed up in single file and passed by the agent without looking at him. Suddenly a deer, or stag, or hart, or maybe it was a roebuck that leapt up in front of them and rushed off into the trees. It was a considerable distance to the highway, and it might well be dawn before they got there.

The countryside, like such a number of things, was what it was, which is to say rilled with streams and declivities that got in the way of travel. They clambered over those obstacles drawing behind them their benefactor still declaiming about race and gender. At one point they happened upon a tumble-down shack with someone living in it, and then the skeleton of a cow who appeared to be dead. Led forward by the light of a sympathetic firefly, they wended their way, respectfully, through an antique graveyard possessed of a certain literary, indeed, Faulknerian ambiance that silenced the members. No longer did they travel in single file; on the contrary, each traveled as he could.

The highway waited just ahead. They raced for it, but only to end up arguing over who had seen it first. That person, it developed, was not however the first actually to have set foot on it causing yet another dispute between the geniuses. Finally, with dawn threatening, they paced along the shoulder of the road for about a hundred yards before having to leap off into the forest when a car came up, stopped, and the driver trained a flashlight on them.

After that they went forward much more cautiously, while at the same time harkening to Reginald's retelling of how the Ten Thousand had found their way back to Sinope on that day. There did seem to be a parked car up ahead which, however, suddenly launched off at top speed as they drew near.

"... or eye color..." the old man called out. "Or sexual business, especially *that*!"

The Town Car, when they located it, was large but old, and one of the doors was missing. It gladdened the members to see a bumper sticker promoting the cause of Southern independence. They were not prepared for the driver, however, an eggplant-colored organism with an egg-shaped head and two eyes of unlike size. He came toward them grinning, his hand held out either for shaking or for the reception of payment. Payment.

"Need 200," he said. "Price of gas just keeps on going up!"

They dug into their pockets for that amount. Fortunately, the group's mycologist had just recently received a letter from his mother and was carrying fifty dollars in his pants.

"I can give you fifty now," he said, "the rest later."

The driver's grin disappeared. He turned sharply and was moving back toward the automobile when the seismologist caught up with him.

"Would you settle for 125?"

"One fifty. That's as low as I can go."

"A hundred and thirty?"

"You offer me 130 and you got a goddamn billionaire with you? Ask *him* for the money!"

"Actually, he's kind of a thrifty person, you understand."

"Yeah, I know. That's how he got to be a billionaire, right?

God, I get tired of hearing that. O.K., how about 140? You can't ask better than that. Nobody can."

They scrambled for the amount, producing a heap of low denomination bills and even a quantity of silver change. It was a relief to find the trunk provided with two pillows, an assortment of blankets, a can of Vienna Sausage, a candle, and some men's magazines.

"He's liable to suffocate in there!"

"Naw, he doesn't need much air. Small as he is."

He was lifted, the old man, into the compartment and his limbs organized into a more or less natural position. At some point along the way he had wet his pants and his hair had leaves in it.

"Well, all right!" the bookbinder said. "Looks real cozy in there!"

"You say so? Elizabeth First had stretching machines more amiable than this."

"Elizabeth? Oh, I don't think she would have done that. Now why don't you just lie down and..."

"Up yours!"

"... do a bit of reading?"

The lid was closed with delicacy but then immediately brought open again when the founder began expostulating even more loudly than before. Under the circumstances they had no alternative but to provide the man a light dosage of valerian that they had hoped not to need.

The return trip should have been at least a little easier than the initial one, and was. Dividing themselves into equal parts, the four scholars took four different trails, ending up at the dormitory in nine, ten, thirteen, and fifty-three minutes respectively. Imagine their dismay upon learning that the physicist had ended his life while they were away.

TWENTY-TWO

Their first response to that tragedy was a gathering of all the members for a performance of Mahler's *Abschied* sung by the chemist. He was a decent tenor, although his overwhelming emotion couldn't fail to subtract from the dignity of the event. In fact, he had gotten all the way to the end of that most beautiful of songs when he came to the word *ewig* and had perforce to leave the stage altogether.

There will be no discussion here of the method used by the physicist to destroy himself.

He had wanted to be buried in the out-of-doors; instead, owing to federal, state, and county regulations, he was interred in a water-tight sarcophagus under the floor of the institution itself. Ornamented in gold leaf with images of the moon and stars and the man's favorite planet, the coffin appeared more comfortable, if slightly narrower, than the trunk of a 1997 Lincoln Town Car. With him he took a small clay figurine of his deceased wife, four books and his extinct cat's favorite pool of yarn. He carried the offprint of a scientific article (authored by himself) that had appeared some years previous in a refereed journal of decent repute. He carried extra shoes, a mobile telephone, and a Babylonian sky chart reproduced on the nether of his coffin lid. He carried a few small objects sealed in a cigar box that might, or might not, have been opened without permission by one of the scholars. Finally, he carried other things as well.

The night was long and drear. His cart laden down with mixed drinks, the supervisor, just as distraught as anyone else, patrolled the corridors. He hoped to offer some sort of consolation by means of the liquors and his own special personality that sometimes served in exigencies of this kind. Suddenly, he crashed into one of the kennels. The hall was that dark. The puppies, most of them sired by the alpha dog called Soames, began at once to howl and moan. Despite that, the supervisor could easily pick up the sound of someone weeping in his cell.

He tapped gently, three times, and then entered without invitation. Holding one of the drinks out in front of him, he approached Egbert's slumped figure, barely visible in the dying light.

"Brace up man!" he said in his therapeutic way. "What, you want somebody to see what a spineless thing you are?"

"Leave me alone! Just leave me alone!"

"You think *this* is a tragedy, what would you have done if *I* had died?"

"Get out."

"Look here, I brought you this top-notch copy of Fioravanti's *Compendium of the rationall secretes of L. Phioravante*. 1582."

"I don't want it."

"You used to want it."

"That was before."

"Look here my man, just what do you think life is after all? O.K., let me explain — life is but a momentary concert of molecules, and it matters scarcely at all if those wee little particles should decide to disassociate."

"Oh? And what if those were *your* molecules?"

"Oh, boy. Well at least I tried. All right, I tell you what, let's take us a ride, you want to? A night ride out into the countryside?"

This time the vehicle was a 1994 Lincoln Town Car with either 167,182, or possibly 267,182 miles on it, depending upon how many times the meter had gone to zero. (He did not believe, the rector, that it could feasibly be 367,182.) It was large enough certainly, although one had first to transfer some hundred weight of volumes from the passenger seat to the rear of the car. The ashtray, it is true, held the remains of a cigarette, a parlous oversight in case of an unannounced county, state, or federal inspection. Nor did the gauge reveal the real quantity of fuel that remained. The other dials were also broken, most of them.

The passenger seat was in wretched condition, with excelsior pouring out. The wipers might or might not have been any good. The heater, of course, was absolutely worthless, and anyone hoping to use it had to endure the uncanny stenches it produced. By contrast, the flooring was whole and had no holes in it. As to the headlights, the less said the better. (They tended to diverge, like the eye beams of a Mantis at prayer. Having diverged, they then lit up the scenery on both sides of the road.) The car had a trunk, of course, although the supervisor was loath to look inside it lest haply it might contain a billionaire.

Three times the engine started and died, forcing the driver to fuddle with the choke for a long time. The snow had largely coagulated and the supervisor must get up "a head of steam" before trying to break out onto the highway.

The road was long and the traffic nonexistent. For some minutes, he drove forward in the mandated direction, his attention fixed on the left-side landscape with its traffic signs and discarded beer cans. The headlight on that side suddenly revealed a coyote glaring back at them with radioactive eyes. And all this time, his passenger continued to whimper while turning slowly through his 1582 book.

"For all we know, Bert," said the preceptor, "Hans is afloat just now in ecstasy. Ecstasy in paradise. A paradise just built for people like him and us."

"No, actually he's already begun to rot."

"A place where all of knowledge is spelled out in the sky."

"Just keep it up, that's right."

"A tour of the universes!"

"Gad. I reckon I can handle my grief without help from you."

"Doubt it. You almost fell apart when your humming bird passed away."

"Oh? And how about if ole Soames kicked the bucket?"

But the supervisor had finished with trying to console the man. Instead, he preferred to turn his attention to the right-hand side of the highway with its hills and quaint little houses that reminded him of the idealized pictures in children's books. Proceeding at about 60 miles an hour, he caught view of a portly man reading a newspaper in a gingerbread house. There was a fire in the hearth and on the mantelpiece four, no five little stand-up photographs of the people who once were important to him. In those days, women used to wear, like, those long dresses, especially the man's mother shown here grinning back shyly at the photographer. But lest these interesting things fall out of ken, the driver slowed and stopped, and then turned back to look at them again.

"Are we going back?" the passenger asked. "Good."

The rector was by no means ready to go all the way home again and especially not so as they were just then coming into a district with some of the best roadside advertisements that he could remember having recently seen. They told of a restaurant close by that served potatoes and fried chicken, and then of an automobile dealership owned by a phlegmatic man (his photograph was shown) of high integrity. Of an insurance agent offering policies of various kind. Better still were the traffic signs directing people to unheard-of destinations whence it was doubtful that any were likely ever to come back again. He came even with an elderly Negro who suddenly turned away to hide his face. Could anything be stranger than the South? No, and after he had covered another half-mile, he caught a fleeting vision of a man in suit and tie standing in the edge of the forest.

TWENTY-THREE

With dangers all around, time went by slowly for the young and instantaneously for the old. And what was "time" after all if not just a *trompe l'oeil* that allowed humans to experience sequentially all the things that had passed in one fell moment long ago? On that theory, the syndics were more and more inclined to come together of evenings in the tea room and read newspapers, or watch old black and white movies from the July/1947–October/1955 period. Some of the members appeared actually to have fallen in love with one of the actresses of those days, a certain *Gail Russell* who would have comprised a perfect wife for any of them. Except that now, instead of admirers, she attracted naught but worms and flies.

It was a melancholy time, that brief interlude known to history as "The Interlude." With just days before the ultimate collapse of their sixteen-year project, the geniuses had begun to tally their findings and send them off to colleagues or university departments or, absurdly, to New York publishers. They might leave the building in twos and threes and, taking the dogs with them, scan the mountains with long-range glasses, always on the lookout for men with carbines. They particularly worried about recent immigrants from sub-Saharan Africa, by common consent, the most enthusiastic regulators in the whole demographic color spectrum. They worried about the helicopters, *black* ones, that hovered overhead. But even more than that, they worried about television and newspaper commentators, a handsome and well-spoken people giving last minute warnings to people like themselves, social reactionaries who still cleaved to certain old social constructs that ought to have expired two generations ago.

A just society can tolerate only so much. Sometimes it becomes necessary "to break a few eggs," as the Attorney General was said to have said. Freedom was one thing, equality another. A blending of individual mental capacities, now genetically achievable, was long overdue. And in truth, the massive inequality in those capacities was probably an even worse source of injustice than inherited estates. Hearing all this on their radios, the membership began resorting more and more often to the pharmacy in Bryson City for aspirin and tranquilizing drugs.

"What's happening up there?" the pharmacist asked. "Y'all aren't getting a just little bit *nervous* are you?" He laughed merrily. "Sooner or later, everybody has to pay the piper. Don't you reckon?"

"I suppose."

"You bet. About time, too."

They gathered that night in the rectory, the entire membership.

"Look, just because we're seeing more and more of them, that doesn't necessarily mean that..."

"Yes it does. That's exactly what it means."

"But we haven't broken any laws for Christ's sakes!"

"Laws? Laws are in the eye of the men on top."

"Which men are those, Karl?"

"Don't know. Nobody knows."

"How do you know they're out there then?"

"Same way I know about Higgs bosons. Never actually seen one of those little suckers you understand."

"Wait a minute, I have to say this: 'Chris knows one hell of a lot more about bosons than you ever could.'"

"You know about 'em?"

"I do not."

"Then how do you know if Chris is right or not? He's got some pretty odd theories."

"We're all of us *odd*, so far as that goes."

"Hold it right there; I'm not going to sit here and let you talk about us that way."

"Well, you could always stand, I guess."

"My God, this coffee is bitter. She's not turning against us, too, is she?"

"*I* made the coffee, thank you very much. Susan quit three days ago."

"She must know something we don't."

"Lots of space there, Howie."

The superintendent brought them back to order. He had not been sleeping well these last nights, the result of too much time patrolling the highway.

"Consider," he said, "that we have two lawyers amongst us. Two. And very good ones. They can defend us against just about anything."

The lawyer called Peterson stood suddenly—he had never stood before—and without being recognized by the chair, said this: "We most certainly can*not* defend us against those diversity charges. Nobody can. Can't be done. Better to take a plea."

"What's the penalty?"

"You don't want to know."

"What about the environmental business? Can they get us on that?"

"Can they get us? Can they get us? They can *always* get us Herb! Just be glad you're as old as you are. And don't have much to lose."

"Oh, I like that. I'm not nearly as old as you!"

"Did I say you were? Did I say you were as old as me? Well, did I?"

The superintendent called them back to order. The geologist, bless his heart, had prepared a basket of iced cupcakes and had begun to hand them out one by one to the intellectuals.

"I'll have that blue one," offered Dwayne. And then, whispering to his nearest seated neighbor, "always been my favorite color, don't you see."

"That's good. But we also have favorite colors Dwayne. Maybe even more than you!"

The supervisor brought them back to order. The little cakes were good certainly, and the following pot of coffee showed improvement. By this time, the clock had moved to just past eleven, time to break out one of the old-time black-and-white films of the 1950s and study the aesthetic of those lost days.

"Shades and shadows," someone said. I like that."

"Yes. And see how they used to dress in those days. No more of that *nostalgie de la boue*, if you take my meaning."

"We take it."

They were silent then. Snow was falling, wind blowing, clouds running. Some had retired to their apartments, abandoning the night's entertainment to those dozen or so personalities who looked upon old films as a sort of hieroglyphic telling of another world.

EPILOGUE

By Thursday, the rector and chief librarian had managed to sequester all the volumes in the A-K range and then two days later, very early in the morning, had arranged for their transfer first to Charleston and then to Paraguay. Not until the last moment did these two men actually leave the building, slipping away at dusk with lightly-packed suitcases. Of the other members, some escaped, some were taken and some, the majority, were not heard from again.

The librarian, as might have been predicted, had accompanied the books to Paraguay. As a person of limited importance in governmental eyes, no effort was made to extradite him back to the United States and, insofar as is known, he passed the following nineteen years organizing and integrating some 75,000 volumes into that country's primary book collection in Asunción. Pensioned off at age seventy-four, he simply disappears from history and nothing more is known of his last years. It can be imagined that he found basic comfort from his income, as small as it undoubtedly was, and from the respect due him for the gentlemanly sort of person that he was. And then, next, one envisions him stretched out quite dead on a cot in a tiny apartment in Latin America.

As to the superintendent himself, nothing was known about him until recently, when a subsidized biography detailing his later career was issued by a small press in Arkansas. According to the author of that account (himself anonymous), the escapee had immediately liquidated the enormous checking account entrusted to him and had assigned the proceeds first to a Bahamian bank and then, 48 hours later, to a "launderer," as such people were called, doing business in Aruba. Even then a full week had to pass before the money (twenty-one and a half million dollars, approximately speaking) was completely safe and could be put to use.

And he did use it, using it to buy a state official and two lawyers who quickly manufactured a new identity for him, one that included honorable service in the Air Force, the earned rank of Eagle Scout and a long career in the advertising industry. So credentialed, he joined a service club and then fell in with a diverse woman who had identity problems of her own. By June they had married and, keeping well apart from each other, divorced in late summer, an action that made their official identities even more plausible than they were.

Came November and he was again in touch with the founder who declined the twenty-million-dollar refund owed to him. They agreed, instead, to search for the surviving members and to set up a new and smaller organization to be hosted by Paraguay's sympathetic ruler, who had already helped them once before.

The fate of the young mathematician was more harsh. Captured immediately, he was given over to a "dark site" experimenting with innovative interrogation procedures. It cannot be imagined that he offered much resistance to the professions he would have encountered there, and it seems probable that he was one of the main sources of the intelligence collected at that place. It is known only that before a full month had gone by, he had been placed under bond with the research arm of a major weapons manufacturer, a listed company where he remained a useful employee right up until his retirement at age 55.

The former professor, a more stubborn type, and his wife were each water-boarded some thirty or thirty-five times, according to the sources, but then did eventually confess to having opposed both in lectures and in spirit the nation's accelerated egalitarianizing efforts. Forced to perform community service in a vibrant neighborhood, he was twice wounded in non-fatal knife attacks and as a consequence juridically separated from his wife. This woman, too, was punished in her own right, although the details remain obscure and in any case lack credibility.

By this date the ophthalmologist had passed less than one full year with the organization, wherefore his readjustment to normal society and to his former practice needed only a short period. Having sacrificed the bulk of his savings to the organization, he right away set out to restore his finances and, it is reported, went so far as to join one of the political parties and even to remarry his former wife. Last seen, he was driving across his yard on a red and white 40 horsepower mowing machine.

Of the dogs, two were immediately liquidated by the first agents to enter the place, while the remaining ones were passed over to trainers who specialized in that breed.

The parrot escaped.

It is true that the one-armed man had already abandoned the organization three days earlier. Bored beyond endurance with the spirit of the place, the moody tenants, and bored, too, with his flagging mistress, he had decamped in early May carrying only a plastic bag with clothes in it and an 8-shot Smith and Wesson .357 magnum revolver. Never seen again, he was reported to have been murdered in Mexico before reaching his fiftieth year.

The founder himself—everyday he was getting older and everyday his money kept on growing. Devoted utterly to his cause, he had succeeded in reuniting in Asunción the seventeen surviving members of his experiment together with four new persons of exceptional brilliance who agreed to work for a better world in which the theory of human equality would once and for all be put aside.

OTHER BOOKS PUBLISHED BY ARKTOS

Sri Dharma Pravartaka Acharya	*The Dharma Manifesto*
Alain de Benoist	*Beyond Human Rights* *Carl Schmitt Today* *The Indo-Europeans* *Manifesto for a European Renaissance* *On the Brink of the Abyss* *The Problem of Democracy* *View from the Right* (vol. 1–3)
Arthur Moeller van den Bruck	*Germany's Third Empire*
Matt Battaglioli	*The Consequences of Equality*
Kerry Bolton	*Revolution from Above* *Yockey: A Fascist Odyssey*
Isac Boman	*Money Power*
Ricardo Duchesne	*Faustian Man in a Multicultural Age*
Alexander Dugin	*Ethnos and Society* *Eurasian Mission* *The Fourth Political Theory* *Last War of the World-Island* *Putin vs Putin* *The Rise of the Fourth Political Theory*
Koenraad Elst	*Return of the Swastika*
Julius Evola	*The Bow and the Club* *Fascism Viewed from the Right* *A Handbook for Right-Wing Youth* *Metaphysics of War* *Notes on the Third Reich* *The Path of Cinnabar* *Recognitions* *A Traditionalist Confronts Fascism*
Guillaume Faye	*Archeofuturism* *Archeofuturism 2.0* *The Colonisation of Europe* *Convergence of Catastrophes* *A Global Coup* *Sex and Deviance* *Understanding Islam* *Why We Fight*
Daniel S. Forrest	*Suprahumanism*

OTHER BOOKS PUBLISHED BY ARKTOS

Andrew Fraser	*Dissident Dispatches* *The WASP Question*
Génération Identitaire	*We are Generation Identity*
Paul Gottfried	*War and Democracy*
Porus Homi Havewala	*The Saga of the Aryan Race*
Rachel Haywire	*The New Reaction*
Lars Holger Holm	*Hiding in Broad Daylight* *Homo Maximus* *Incidents of Travel in Latin America* *The Owls of Afrasiab*
Alexander Jacob	*De Naturae Natura*
Jason Reza Jorjani	*Prometheus and Atlas* *World State of Emergency*
Roderick Kaine	*Smart and SeXy*
Lance Kennedy	*Supranational Union and New Medievalism*
Peter King	*Here and Now* *Keeping Things Close*
Ludwig Klages	*The Biocentric Worldview* *Cosmogonic Reflections*
Pierre Krebs	*Fighting for the Essence*
Stephen Pax Leonard	*Travels in Cultural Nihilism*
Pentti Linkola	*Can Life Prevail?*
H. P. Lovecraft	*The Conservative*
Charles Maurras	*The Future of the Intelligentsia & For a French Awakening*
Michael O'Meara	*Guillaume Faye and the Battle of Europe* *New Culture, New Right*
Brian Anse Patrick	*The NRA and the Media* *Rise of the Anti-Media* *The Ten Commandments of Propaganda* *Zombology*
Tito Perdue	*Morning Crafts* *Philip* *William's House* (vol. 1–4)

OTHER BOOKS PUBLISHED BY ARKTOS

Raido	*A Handbook of Traditional Living*
Steven J. Rosen	*The Agni and the Ecstasy* *The Jedi in the Lotus*
Richard Rudgley	*Barbarians* *Essential Substances* *Wildest Dreams*
Ernst von Salomon	*It Cannot Be Stormed* *The Outlaws*
Sri Sri Ravi Shankar	*Celebrating Silence* *Know Your Child* *Management Mantras* *Patanjali Yoga Sutras* *Secrets of Relationships*
Troy Southgate	*Tradition & Revolution*
Oswald Spengler	*Man and Technics*
Tomislav Sunic	*Against Democracy and Equality* *Postmortem Report* *Titans are in Town*
Hans-Jürgen Syberberg	*On the Fortunes and Misfortunes of Art in Post-War Germany*
Abir Taha	*Defining Terrorism: The End of Double Standards* *The Epic of Arya* (2nd ed.) *Nietzsche's Coming God, or the Redemption of the Divine* *Verses of Light*
Bal Gangadhar Tilak	*The Arctic Home in the Vedas*
Dominique Venner	*For a Positive Critique* *The Shock of History*
Markus Willinger	*A Europe of Nations* *Generation Identity*

CPSIA information can be obtained
at www.ICGtesting.com
Printed in the USA
LVHW03s0501090818
586468LV00001B/13/P

9 781912 079858